Tales of the Were
Grizzly Cove

The Luck of the Shifters

BIANCA D'ARC

This book is a work of fiction. The names, characters, places, and incidents are products of the writer's imagination or have been used fictitiously and are not to be construed as real. Any resemblance to persons, living or dead, actual events, locale or organizations is entirely coincidental.

ISBN: 1543239935
ISBN-13: 978-1543239935

DEDICATION

With many thanks to Peggy and Dave for hunting down the typo fairies, as well as my awesome editor, Jess, who keeps all the commas in line.

Much love to my family, especially Dad, who cheers on my word counts, though he'll never read any of these books.

And special thanks to my late bff Mary, who taught me all I know about the Emerald Isle and those who trace their ancestry to it, but were born elsewhere.

CHAPTER ONE

Moira Kinkaid liked what she'd seen so far of Grizzly Cove. She had arrived the day before and had met with the mayor and town council straight away. They were all strong bears, with lots of "real world" experience, according to her cousin. She knew that meant they were Special Operators who had been proven in battle time and again.

She respected strength and wisdom equally, and these bears seemed to have both.

She'd been around lion shifters most of her life. Clan Kinkaid was an odd one—half lion, half selkie—through an odd circumstance of fate. One of the Kinkaid ancestors had traveled to Africa and fallen for the daughter of the lion Alpha. Their children had turned out to be lions, for the most part, but the selkie side of the family had reasserted itself in recent years.

Moira was a selkie, with more than her fair share of magical power. In fact, she was one of the most powerful of the Clan's selkie shifters. Cousin to the Alpha, she was used as a troubleshooter in all sorts of situations where delicacy was needed. Both in business and in magic, she had a way of flying under the radar of her opponents and coming out the victor. She was also really good at untangling difficult situations without drawing blood on either side. It was one of her many talents.

When she'd arrived in Grizzly Cove the day before, she knew she'd been a bit of a surprise to the bear Alpha. No doubt he'd been expecting one of her burly male relatives. The ones who'd been the driving force behind the US Navy's development of the SEAL teams back in the 1960's. They'd thought it was both ironic and fitting that the Navy would call the teams SEALs, never really knowing that the men they employed—especially those chosen few back in the early years—had really been seal shifters.

Now, of course, there were small groups of Special Forces soldiers all under the command of Admiral Morrow, himself a magical water sprite. He ran interference between the human side of the armed forces and the special teams of Army Rangers, Green Berets, Navy SEALs, Force Recon and other commandos who had a little something extra in their arsenal of talents and abilities.

Few people knew about it, but Moira was highly placed in her Clan, and her cousin kept her informed. He was a good Alpha, even if he was a lion. He treated everyone with equality and promoted based on skill and ability rather than nepotism or favoritism.

The bear Alpha of Grizzly Cove seemed to be cut of the same cloth, and she knew from her pre-mission briefing that he had led the Special Forces team that had retired and chosen to settle together here, in this cove. They were mostly bears of different types and had invited other bear shifters to join them.

Bears, being more magical by nature than most other shifters, usually didn't congregate in one place, so this entire town was something of a social experiment. The unprecedented concentration of magical power had attracted Others too. Both good folk—like the vampire Master of Seattle, Hiram Abernathy—and bad things, like the leviathan that now threatened the coast.

It was the leviathan that had caused the influx of merfolk into the cove. The bear Alpha could have turned them away, but had instead opened the floodgates, welcoming them with open arms. Three of his bears were now mated to mermaids and very happy, from all accounts. The mer pod was setting up housekeeping in the waters of the cove, and the bears were building special accommodations for them on land, as well.

Moira had been pleased to see the way the two very different shifter populations were blending and working together in the town. She was very used to that sort of thing in her Clan, but it wasn't common anywhere else.

She was taking her time getting to know these people. It wouldn't do to ride into town and try to take over. Moira knew better than that. She had to see what she could contribute here, first, before she let loose with her selkie viewpoints and knowledge—which were usually quite different from those held by land shifters...even those in her own Clan.

So she was walking the beach, trying to get the lay of the land. She'd never been to this part of the Pacific coastline before, and she was enjoying learning the timing of the tides and the personality of the waters here. It was a lovely place.

Except for the drunk passed out on the beach a few yards away.

Moira sighed. It never failed. There was always one drunkard in the group—even though it took enormous amounts of alcohol to affect a shifter. Their metabolisms made it difficult for most drugs or other substances to affect them, so a person really had to be dedicated to get and maintain a stupor.

She knew many of the residents here were veterans, so she felt a little pang of compassion, even though she didn't know this particular shifter's story. Yet.

She couldn't just leave him where he was. The tide was coming in, and he was face down on the beach. If he didn't wake up soon, he'd most likely drown. Even this far away, she could catch a faint bit of his scent. What wasn't soaked in alcohol was furry, not fishy, so leaving him where the water would cover him wasn't a good idea. With a resigned cadence to her feet, she marched over to the unconscious man.

Moira wasn't sure how he would react, so she prodded him with her toe first, hoping to wake him. When he didn't respond, she pushed a little harder, flipping him onto his back.

Her breath caught when she saw his face for the first time. Hard, angular features were slack in sleep, but he was a handsome devil. His hair was unruly and naturally curled. It was dark now, with moisture absorbed from the sand, but she saw hints of gold in the tousled curls.

He wasn't a giant of a man like the other bear shifters who lived here. No, he was built more like a muscular, fit, totally hot human, which suited her just fine because she was rather petite for a selkie.

And why in the world was she thinking about this strange man's stature in relation to her own? Moira shook herself. She'd come here to do a job, not get mixed up with some sad case shifter who drank too much.

Now that she was closer to him, the scent of alcohol and fur mixed with…eucalyptus? Just faintly, but it was there. Maybe he liked cough drops? Though, as far as she knew, shifters didn't really get casual colds the way humans did. The good-looking guy on the sand at her feet was a puzzle, that was for sure.

She touched him with her toe again, trying to nudge him awake. She didn't want to get too close in case he woke up disoriented and took a swipe at her. She'd startled awake a few lion shifters from her Clan in the past and had learned to approach cautiously.

A faint groan was her reward. Maybe he was waking up.

"Hey, mister, you're going to get hit by the tide if you don't get up soon."

Another growling moan sounded, a bit louder this time. She nudged him with her toe again.

"Oi! Leave off," he growled, the few words tinged with a thick accent. She couldn't be sure, but he didn't sound like one of her cousins from County Kerry in

Ireland. He didn't sound American, either.

"Hey, mister, get up or you're going to get wet in…" She looked at the approaching line of sea foam. As a water shifter, she was a good judge of the tide, and it was coming in fast now. Yeah, the drunk guy was going to get wet. She almost sighed. Here it came… "Three, two, one," she counted down, watching the inevitable as the water sloshed over the man's sneakers and up to mid-thigh.

"Shite, that's cold!" The man skittered away from the retreating tide, suddenly mobile. Moira wanted to laugh, but refrained, merely following his progress with a smile she couldn't repress.

He ended up a short way up the dune, sitting on his butt with his knees drawn up and his arms resting over them, his head hung low as he dragged his hands through his shaggy hair. His jeans were wet from the middle of his muscular thighs down to his scuffed sneakers, and he wore a denim jacket over an Army green T-shirt.

"Do you need me to call anyone?" she asked tentatively, moving a bit closer. She didn't want to leave him out here like this if there was something she could do to help. He was in sorry shape for a shifter.

Bloodshot blue eyes met hers. Then, they narrowed as he took her in.

"You're not a bear, and you're not a fish," he said, looking her up and down. "And you're not human or witch. You're a shifter, but what sort?" He sniffed in her direction—rather rudely, she thought—and then, his face went even paler, if that was possible. "It can't be…"

"You look like you've seen a ghost," she couldn't help but remark.

"Maybe I have. Or maybe the selkies have sent you to take their revenge on my worthless hide once and for all." He lowered his gaze, dipped his head, and she thought maybe she'd glimpsed tears in his eyes before he'd hidden them. His words were troubling.

"I'm a selkie, but I've come here at the invitation of the Alpha to consult on the leviathan problem. Who are you that you recognize my kind? And why do you think we'd seek revenge against you?"

She tried to put a bit of firmness into her voice. Her brothers were so much better at intimidation than she would ever be, but she'd learned a thing or two growing up with them.

"Because of the boy," he whispered, lifting his head to stare into the approaching waves as if they held the answer.

"What are you talking about?" she asked when he hadn't said anything further for a while.

She'd waited to see if he would go on with his cryptic words, but he seemed to be stuck in a memory, staring straight ahead. Perhaps he was reliving something or seeing something only he could see.

Or perhaps she'd had the misfortune to run across a loony-tunes bear shifter on this stretch of desolate beach. Well, she could always run into the surf and disappear under the waves if he turned violent. Bears might be good swimmers, but she'd bet they could never out-swim a seal shifter.

"My name is Moira. What's yours?" She tried a different tack when he didn't answer.

That seemed to get a response. He blinked and turned his head to gaze up at her as if seeing her for the first time. Maybe the alcohol he'd soaked his head in was starting to burn off a bit. His glassy eyes seemed to take a moment to focus.

"I'm Seamus," he answered, a little bit of a twang to his words that didn't sound Irish to her trained ears.

"Sure and with a name like Seamus, ya aren't from the old country?" She put on the best imitation of her Irish cousins' brogues she could manage.

His eyes narrowed. "Neither are you, sheila, though you claim a name just as Irish as mine."

"You're an Aussie!" She snapped her fingers, smiling. It was the use of the term *sheila* that had given him away, though she suspected he'd done it on purpose.

He tapped his nose, then pointed at her, one corner of his mouth lifted in a smile. Her breath caught. When Seamus smiled... Whoa, momma. And that had been a weak smile at best. She wondered what a full-wattage, all-out smile would do. Maybe cause an earthquake? Some sort of seismic shift?

She shook her head at her own fancifulness and crouched down to be at eye level with him. Seamus seemed to be in trouble, and she wanted to help. She'd help any being who needed it. The fact that he was drop-dead-gorgeous really had nothing to do with it. Nope. No, siree.

"Can I buy you a cup of coffee, Seamus?" she asked gently.

He rubbed a dirty hand over his scruffy face. He hadn't shaved in a bit, and his strong jaw was covered with fine golden bristles.

"I look that bad, eh?" He looked left and right, seeming to assess the situation in which he'd awoken and then shook his head. "I probably smell worse than I feel. I'm sorry, Moira. You're not catching me on a good day."

"That's okay," she assured him. "We all have bad ones every now and again." She stood, and he followed suit, a little unsteady on his feet. "The offer of coffee stands. There's a bakery in town that serves hot drinks and sandwiches. I was just heading back that way." She lied about her destination, but it was a socially-acceptable white lie, so she figured it didn't count.

"I appreciate the polite fiction," he said with quiet dignity and a rueful twist of his lips. "But how about I buy you the coffee, Moira? I don't need charity."

"It wasn't—" she protested, but he cut her off.

"I thank you for the offer, and if you really want to help, you'll do me the favor of going into the bakery and getting my order to go for me. Those women don't like me, and I try not to darken their door any more than necessary, but they do make some fine grub." He seemed to be sobering up right before her eyes.

He fumbled in his pockets for a moment before pulling out a wad of cash. He peeled off a fifty and held it out toward her. Who carried that kind of cash around with them? Her suspicions rose again. Was he some sort of criminal, dealing in large denomination bills?

"I'm on the level." He seemed to read her hesitancy for what it was. "You can ask the Alpha bear. He knows my story, and they're letting me stay. I've been out of circulation for a while, and I want to stay under the radar, so Big John helped me access my bank account as anonymously as possible, and I'm using cash-only for the next few months, until I'm sure I got away clean."

"Away from what?" They started walking back down the beach, toward town. She kept a couple of yards distant from him, just in case she still needed to make a run for it.

"I suppose you'll hear it from someone in town, so I might as well tell you myself. I was being held prisoner in a private zoo in my other form. I managed to break out, but I'm not sure if the people who were holding me will come after me or not. Big John has agreed to give me sanctuary."

"That's…pretty awful," she told him, her heart going out to the stoic shifter who had to have gone through some pretty horrific times, if what he said was true. She'd check with the Alpha before buying the entire sob story, but she was willing to give Seamus the benefit of the doubt for now.

"Yeah, well…" He cleared his throat as if uncomfortable. "I don't need any sympathy. I'm out now, and so are the others, as far as I know. We got out and split up. The others probably had families to go back to in the States, but I'm not from around here. I didn't want to chance getting on a plane. There'd be a trail of my identity leading back to Oz…and my family. Plus there's the little matter of not having a passport. They didn't bring me into the country legally, so I don't have any I.D. to help me get back home."

"I can see how that would present a problem," she allowed.

Of course, with Clan Kinkaid's resources, she could easily get the use of a private jet that would take him anywhere he wanted to go, with no record of his trip. She'd save telling him that for later…if he turned out to be telling the truth.

"So tell me, why are you persona non grata in the bakery?" she asked, hoping to feel out Seamus a bit more.

"When I first came to town, I was…well…as you just found me. Drunk. Stupid. It's been a hell of a year." He swiped his hand through his tousled curls and sighed. "I went into the bakery looking for food and thinking that the entire town was made up of shifters. I didn't realize the ladies that owned the shop were human. Or that they didn't know about shifters. I sort of…" He sighed again. "I'm not too proud of my behavior. I got a bit belligerent, and when Sheriff Brody got all up in my face, I shifted. Right there in the middle of the bakery. In front of the clueless human woman who ended up mating the sheriff."

Moira shook her head. "Wow," she said finally. "You really know how to pick your battles. He was protecting his mate, and you got into a dominance fight with him right there in the middle of his mate's territory? Which one of you won?"

"If it's up to me, I'd say neither. But

Brody's bigger. Hell, they're *all* bigger than me. But I've got it where it counts, sweetheart." He threw her a casual wink and that devastating half-smile. Damn.

The man had just admitted to being smaller than all the other bears, and yet somehow, she sensed he didn't feel any the less for his stature. In fact, he seemed about as Alpha as any of the badass Alphas she knew. There was something strange going on here. She just couldn't put her finger on what it was.

"So you can see why I don't like to darken the ladies' door if I can help it. It's going to take a while for my entrance into town to be forgotten."

They were nearing the more populated area at the apex of the cove. Main Street ran right past the edge of the water, and the infamous bakery was just across the street. There was little to no traffic.

"Will you get the order to go for me, Moira?" Seamus turned toward her, holding out the fifty again and giving her a hopeful expression that would've looked at home on a cocker spaniel.

She laughed and plucked the fifty from his hand. "What do you want, Seamus? And

I warn you—I won't buy you anything alcoholic. You've had more than enough of that for one day."

He shook his head, chuckling. "Aye, you're right on that score." He then proceeded to describe the giant sandwiches they made in the bakery and the two he wanted for himself. He also instructed her to pick up a large black coffee for him and anything she wanted for herself. His treat.

Moira went across the street, still shaking her head at the crazy Aussie shifter she'd just encountered. She saw him sit on one of the picnic tables set far up the sand, just next to the road as she entered the bakery. Maybe she could get the story about him out of the ladies in the bakery, just to double check that his farfetched tale was true. She was new in town, after all, and she didn't know these people. She had to keep her eyes open and her senses sharp.

Not only was she here to help with the sea monster problem, but she was also acting as Clan Kinkaid's forward scout in this instance. Her report on this town would decide if the Kinkaids had any more to do with Grizzly Cove. They were on trial here, with her, and they probably didn't even realize it.

The Kinkaid billions were quietly spread around to various shifter concerns all over the world. Samson Kinkaid, the lion Alpha, liked to help others where he could, and he'd sent Moira here with the instruction to discover what Grizzly Cove was all about. If it was as good in reality as it looked in theory, Kinkaid might just be ready to infuse some cash into the town. If not, then she'd go back home, and the bears would never be the wiser.

CHAPTER TWO

As luck would have it, all three of the sisters who owned and operated the bakery were on hand when Moira went in. She'd met Nell, the eldest, briefly when she'd arrived in town. Nell was mated to the town's sheriff, Brody Chambers. She'd been seated with the witch, Ursula, mate to the Alpha bear, John Marshall, who'd been there to welcome Moira in her official capacity as Alpha female.

Nell had invited her over to the bakery for coffee, after the official meeting in town hall, and Moira had been introduced to Ashley, the middle sister, who was mated to the town's only lawyer, Tom Masdan. Moira had dossiers on all the players and knew that Ashley was also an attorney, though there'd been some trouble at her last job in the human world that had caused her to leave under a cloud.

Moira wouldn't betray her knowledge of things that were probably meant to be kept private, but it helped to know the backgrounds of the people she was dealing with in cases like this. These folks had no idea the Kinkaid Alpha was thinking of investing in their town, so they would behave in their normal manner, not trying to butter up the Kinkaid rep with special treatment. That's exactly what Moira wanted. It would make her two-fold job a lot easier. The main purpose of her visit was to help in whatever way she could with the leviathan problem, of course, but her Alpha wasn't one to let an opportunity go to waste.

Moira greeted the two sisters she'd already met with smiles and was introduced to the third sister, Tina, who was mated to a Cajun black bear named Zak Flambeau. Zak, Kinkaid had learned, was in partnership with the vampire Master of Seattle, Hiram Abernathy, to build a new restaurant in

Grizzly Cove. Some might think it odd that a vampire would invest as a silent partner in a restaurant, but it really was a good way to maintain his façade of humanity.

It was the restaurant deal—which was by no means a secret—that had piqued Kinkaid's interest in the town. That, and the influx of mer into the cove, had indicated to the lion Alpha that something—possibly something extraordinary—was happening in the new town.

Kinkaid knew Hiram to be an upstanding Master of the bloodletters in his area, and all reports about him said that he was just and fair to those under him. If he was interested in Grizzly Cove, then it was worth Kinkaid's time to send someone to take a first-hand look. The request for selkie help on their sea monster problem that had come directly from the Alpha bear, John Marshall, had been an opportunity the Kinkaid Alpha could not pass up. So he'd sent Moira, who also happened to be one of his top executives.

Nobody in Grizzly Cove knew that, of course. In fact, Moira could count on one hand the number of people in the world who knew her true position in her Clan. Her brothers were all highly placed, of course, but she was seen as a small, weak female of her kind, and she was often underestimated. Which was fine with her. It served her purposes and let her fly under the radar, even within her own Clan sometimes.

What she'd seen of Grizzly Cove so far impressed her. All except for drunken Seamus, waiting for her at the picnic table across the street while Ashley and Tina made his sandwiches. Nell saw the direction of Moira's gaze as she checked on him and nudged her elbow.

"Seamus is kind of a mess," Nell said, opening the conversation. "Have you met him yet?"

Moira saw no reason to withhold information. "I found him passed out on the beach not twenty minutes ago. I'm getting sandwiches for him, because he said he tries to avoid coming in here if he can. Apparently, you don't like him?" Moira turned her questioning gaze on Nell, waiting to see what the bakery owner would say to that.

"Oh, for goodness' sake." Nell seemed genuinely frustrated. "I'll admit he scared the bejeezus out of me when he first came to town, but he's welcome in the bakery. There aren't a lot of places to buy food here yet, and I wouldn't turn anyone away." Now Nell looked concerned as she gazed across the street at the disheveled shifter. "Was he drunk again?"

"Yeah," Moira admitted. "The tide was coming in, and his legs got soaked, but it woke him up. He seems to be sobering fast now that he's awake."

"Poor devil. He really is a wreck. Brody told me a little bit about what happened to him, because of the way he frightened me, but I'm not sure if even John knows the full story." Nell bit her lower lip as if worried about Seamus's welfare.

"Did he really shift right in front of you?" Moira dared to ask.

Nell looked at her in surprise. "He told you about that?" When Moira nodded, Nell shook her head and sighed. "I was clueless about shifters. Turns out my sisters had known for weeks, but they didn't let me in on their little discovery for fear I'd make us all move." Nell smiled ruefully at that memory. "But when Seamus went furry, and then Brody did the same… I was shocked, I can tell you. It all turned out okay, and

Seamus apologized. In fact, he's apologized just about every time I've seen him since then. I can tell he still feels bad about the fright he gave me. I just wish he wouldn't drink so much. At the rate he's going, he's going to pickle himself before too much longer."

"He told me he was held prisoner. Is that true?" Moira was beginning to think the drunk shifter was on the level, but she would have to back up his story with other sources. She'd learned to be cautious in her profession.

"Sadly, yes," Nell confirmed. "Our town doctor, Sven Olafsson, treated him when he first got here. Sven told Brody the condition Seamus was in at that time tended to support his story. Brody's been trying to track down the culprit who held him, and any other shifters who might have escaped and need help, but so far, he hasn't had much luck. Of course, we've been a little distracted with all the mer moving in and the leviathan problem."

"I don't doubt it," Moira agreed. "You've got your hands full here."

"John said that he never envisioned the town becoming a haven for refugee shifters, but he's glad it's here to help those who need it. Maybe once we get the sea monster thing under control, we can go back to being a normal town… Well, normal for a town full of shifters pretending to be an artists' colony. I still shake my head at that. How Big John ever came up with an idea like that… And my husband keeps right on with his chainsaws, carving bears out of hunks of tree trunks. And people still keep buying them. It boggles the mind."

"They're all self-portraits," Tina piped in, placing the to-go order on top of the counter. "At least that's what Zak says." She smiled at her older sister and turned to accept the fifty-dollar bill Moira held out. "The guys all tease Brody about how he only ever does one bear—himself. They want to know when he'll branch out and do portraits of the other guys in town. This Seamus's money?" Tina looked speculatively from the bag to the picnic table across the street and back again to Moira.

"Yeah. He sent me to get the sandwiches for him," Moira admitted.

"I wish he wouldn't do that," Ashley said, looking across the street, her brows drawn together in concern. "He's welcome here. I hate that he thinks we don't like him."

Tina handed the fifty-dollar bill back to Moira, then added a bag of dessert pastries to the bag with the sandwiches. "It's on the house today," Tina said. "Tell him, next time, he should come in himself, and I'll fix him one of Zak's special off-menu platters. We don't make those for just anybody."

Moira knew Zak was, from all accounts, an accomplished chef, and it wouldn't be long before his restaurant opened. It was going to be in the new building going up right next to the bakery, in fact.

"I'll tell him. Just..." Moira paused, hoping the other ladies would catch on and spill more information about Seamus. "Is there anything I should know about him? I mean, he's safe, right?" She was small for a shifter, which worked in her favor most of the time. Even among these human women, her smaller stature seemed to bring out their protective instincts.

"Oh, he's okay," Nell said quickly. "Just messed up about what happened to him, but he's not dangerous or anything. He wouldn't hurt anybody."

"Except maybe himself," Tina added, her tone sad.

"But he's a bear, and all," Moira added, hoping to elicit more information.

Her words didn't get the reaction she'd expected. All three women looked at her with varying expressions of surprise.

"He's not—" Tina began, but Nell cut her off.

"He's not like the others," Nell stated with quiet dignity. "But it's up to him to disclose how and why. I can say that he's safe enough for you to be around in either of his forms. You're a shifter, right? And from what Brody said, you're a swimmer. You can handle Seamus."

"I still can't really get used to being in a town where everyone knows about shifters," Moira marveled. It was unique in her experience to be talking so openly about her other half in the middle of a bakery. With regular humans, no less.

Of course, all three sisters were now shifter mates, so that was the big difference. They weren't just regular humans anymore. They'd been adopted into the bear Clan.

The town probably wouldn't always be this way. If they got more human tourists coming through—which was bound to happen sooner or later with all the art the town was starting to produce—they'd have to be more circumspect. But for now, it was pretty darn cool to be able to talk freely, out in the open.

"I'm still not used to all this either, to tell you the truth, but Brody says, in a few years, I won't jump every time he goes furry." Nell laughed, and the others joined her.

"I put your sandwich in there too, and here are the drinks," Ashley said, handing over a cup carrier with two large to-go cups in it. "Napkins and plastic cutlery are in the bag too."

"Thanks," Moira said. "Can I at least pay you for my share?" she asked, feeling a bit strange about taking all this away and not paying for it.

"Consider it a welcome-to-town gift," Nell said as she headed back around the counter. "I hope we'll see more of you while you're here."

"That's very kind of you. Thanks," Moira said, meaning it. "I'm meeting Urse and Mel here tomorrow morning, as a matter of fact, so I'll see you then."

Seamus wondered what he'd gotten himself into as he watched the women in the bakery as furtively as he could. He tried so hard to keep a low profile around the three human sisters. He was embarrassed beyond belief by what he'd done when he'd first come to town. It was unforgivable, the way he'd frightened that poor sheila. His mum had taught him better than that. She'd be appalled if she knew what her baby boy had done to terrorize that poor woman.

Thankfully, it had all worked out, but if Nell hadn't turned out to be a shifter's mate, Seamus would've been in even more serious trouble. Betraying the existence of shifters to regular humans was a big no-no. It was something he'd been raised to avoid since he was a child.

He'd learned first-hand how dangerous humans could be when they found out about shifters. He'd been kept prisoner in that menagerie by humans, frozen in his animal form for months, forced to live as the animal that shared his soul, but in a terrible confinement that had nearly smothered his spirit.

They'd taunted him day and night, trying to get him to shift so they could catch it on film. And he wasn't the only one. There'd been others in that dark hole with him. All kinds of others. Some were just animals, but a precious few had been shifters. There had been a lioness and a seal youngster, and a few more besides. But Seamus had seen those two on more than one occasion, and they'd each given him the nod—after a first startled glance—that meant they were standing strong and staying in animal form to deny their captors the satisfaction of getting what they wanted.

What had ultimately become of the lioness, Seamus didn't know, but the boy…

Seamus cringed when he thought about the boy.

"Here we go." Moira's bright voice intruded on his reverie. Thank the Goddess.

Seamus didn't need to go down memory lane again. He'd only just sobered up. Thinking about the boy made Seamus want the oblivion of drink…so he could forget.

He looked up to find Moira sitting across from him at the picnic table, already setting out the sandwiches and drinks like a good little hostess. She really was cute as a button and sexy as hell. A strange contradiction, but somehow, for her, it worked.

"The ladies in the bakery said today's feast was on the house." She slid the fifty-dollar bill he'd given her earlier across the table, tucking it under his sandwich.

He didn't want it back, but he'd probably need every last penny he'd been able to secure to stay under the radar for as long as possible. Still, he didn't like the idea of accepting charity, or taking from the three human women who ran the bakery where he'd messed up so badly. He looked across the street, pursing his lips. He'd have to make this up to them somehow. Seamus O'Leary always paid his way.

"They shouldn't have done that," he said finally, focusing back on the table and pocketing the fifty as calmly as he could. He didn't like it, but he'd learned over the past months that, sometimes, you had to endure things you didn't like in order to keep existing.

"They feel badly that you won't go in there. They said you're welcome in the bakery and that you should come in whenever you like. All's forgiven, apparently."

Seamus looked at his companion, trying to gauge her expression, but she was busy taking a bite out of a sandwich that was almost too large for her. It would have been comical except for the fact that watching her eat was turning him on.

Shite! Seamus hadn't even looked at a woman with desire in months. It had been a long dry spell speckled with trauma and emotional turmoil. The last thing he'd been thinking of was women or sex. But now, faced with this small, oddly enchanting shifter female, he felt a strong attraction smack him right between the eyes.

And damned if she wasn't familiar to him. Oh, he'd never met her before, but she smelled of sea and fur, just like…just like the boy had done, back in the menagerie. She was a seal shifter—a selkie, like the legends out of the old country.

Irish myth abounded with tales of selkies caught on shore when a cunning human found the hiding places of their seal skins and stole them. The idea was simple: steal the seal's skin, force the selkie to stay human…and with you…until you let down your guard and he or she found the hiding place of their skin, stole it back and took off into the waves, never to be seen again.

Reality was a bit different from those old legends. For one thing, selkies didn't take off their skins like fur coats and leave them lying around. No, selkies were shifters, just like any other shifter, except they had a lot more magic and were reputed to be very rare.

The boy had told Seamus, when they'd escaped together, that his name was Eamon. A good Irish name for a thoroughly American lad. Seamus had no doubt young Eamon could trace his lineage back to Ireland. Just like Seamus could.

Of course, Seamus's Irish ancestors hadn't been immigrants exactly. No, they'd been forced to sail to Botany Bay, as it was called back then. Shipped off to Australia with the other convicts. Only Seamus's family had fallen in with the Australian natives and mated with shifters. Generation after generation had inherited the native animal spirits, the indigenous heritage and the gift for blarney. And, in Seamus's case at least, a liking for Scotch whiskey.

Rather than say anything, Seamus decided to shelve the talk and eat up. His stomach was as empty as his head, and the sandwiches were calling his name.

They ate in silence for a while. Moira was easy to be around, he was discovering, and she was definitely easy on the eyes. With pretty dark hair and pale skin, she had the deep ocean blue eyes and complexion of what was known as the *dark Irish*.

At length, she finished with her sandwich and started cleaning up the wrappings that might otherwise blow away in the breeze. She sipped her coffee and dug into the bag, coming up with a smaller bag—this one filled with pastries.

"Tina sent these along for you, but I suppose you can spare one for a stranger in town, right?" She sent him a comical look, blinking her big eyes at him.

"You're more than welcome," he told her. If she looked at him like that, she could have pretty much anything she wanted, just for making him feel like smiling.

Lord knew, there'd been precious little to smile about lately.

"So…" She gestured with the pastry in her hand after taking a bite. "With a name like Seamus, your last name probably begins with a *Mc*, am I right?"

Her impertinent question startled a laugh out of him. "Almost. It's O'Leary," he said, holding his hand out across the picnic table, as was only polite when introducing yourself to your rescuer. "Seamus O'Leary from Sydney, Australia."

"Moira Kinkaid, from Houston, Texas. Well, I live there now, but I was born in New York," she replied as they shook hands.

When his skin touched hers, there was a little spark that he could have sworn arced between them. A small zap of magic that wasn't the normal thing at all. He wanted to keep holding her hand and explore the feeling more, but politeness dictated he had to let go after a reasonable period. He'd held her a shade too long already. She tugged slightly, and he let her loose, remembering his manners.

The animal inside him that had been abused didn't want to have *manners*. It wanted to sniff the female. It wanted to touch her and mount her and make her theirs.

Whoa. Where had *that* come from? Seamus shook his head. He really had been in his animal form a bit too long. It wasn't good to let either side have that much control for that lengthy a period, but he hadn't had any other options, stuck in the menagerie.

Scratch that. He'd had options, but all of them had been bad. He'd decided early on it was better to lose his humanity and stay furry for the rest of his miserable life than give his captors the satisfaction of having broken him. He might have been imprisoned, but his spirit had remained strong. The beast side of him had seen to that.

"Pleased to meet you officially, Moira Kinkaid," Seamus said, testing her name out on his tongue. It felt good there. Tasted right. But there was something… "Wait a minute. Kinkaid? Are you the representative from Clan Kinkaid everybody's been expecting?"

"That I am," she agreed with a friendly smile.

"And here I am making a grand impression on you. What must you think of the town, with me passed out on the beach?" He shook his head with a rueful expression. "My apologies, Moira. Please don't judge this place by my actions. They let me stay, but I'm not really one of them. I'm sort of a charity case around here."

CHAPTER THREE

"That's no way to talk, O'Leary. We all have down times, and this just happens to be one of yours. Or maybe… You *were* down, but you're on your way back up again with the indulgence of the folks here. Given time to heal from your experience, I don't doubt you'll straighten out your path in no time. You've already made friends here, whether you realize it or not." She nodded toward the bakery across the street.

"Moira, with all due respect, you don't really know what you're talking about. I'm not even a real bear in their eyes. Hell, technically I'm a marsupial. I'm the only shifter in this town that actually gets smaller when I change."

"Wait... What *are* you?" Moira regretted the question the moment it left her lips. It was the height of rudeness to ask a shifter that question. It just wasn't done in polite circles. "I'm sorry—" she began, but he waved her off.

"I'm a koala. Didn't the gals in the bakery tell you? The grizzlies have been having a good laugh at my expense ever since I got here." He looked like he wanted to bolt. He seemed angry and frustrated and unsure what to do with those volatile emotions.

"I hope not." She decided to be straight with him. "If you know about my Clan, you know it's one of the richest in the world. Our Alpha likes to spread the wealth sometimes, but if these grizzlies are uncivilized enough to make you—a fellow shifter—unwelcome here, then they won't be seeing a penny of Kinkaid support. I can assure you of that." She felt righteous indignation rise to cover the fact that she'd just blown her own cover.

She never did that! At least, she'd never done that before while on a mission for the Alpha. What had come over her?

"No." He seemed to calm a bit. "No. I don't want to hurt the people of this town. There are good folks here. It's me who's the problem."

"Seamus…" Her heart went out to the mixed-up man.

It was clear to her that Seamus was dealing with some pretty heavy stuff. Insecurities and events that had scarred him badly.

But Moira knew something about being vulnerable because you were smaller than everybody else. She got up and moved around to his side of the picnic table, taking a seat right beside him.

"Seamus…" Her voice softened. "I've never said this aloud before, but everyone thinks I'm the runt of the Kinkaid Clan."

That admission cost her in pride, but he needed to hear it. His gaze rose to meet hers, and she saw the turmoil deep in his eyes. She took a deep breath and forged on.

"Look at me." She held her arms out to her sides, inviting him to take a good look. "As a human, I'm small. As a seal, well, I'm not even close to the size of most of my fellow selkies. And half my Clan is populated by giant scary-assed lions. The big joke when

I was growing up was that one of the lion cubs was going to try to eat me, but I wasn't even big enough to make a good snack."

She laughed ruefully. The others hadn't realized how much their teasing had hurt her. For all that she was a shifter, she still had a sensitive soul. Words could hurt, and she'd learned the hard way, they often did.

"But my Alpha trusts me. Most of the Clan has no idea that I'm one of his most highly-placed business operatives. I earned my place with brains and determination, but for a long time, I just wallowed in self-pity. I had to realize I wasn't going to be like the others. I had to be better than them. Different. I had to forge my own path, and at long last, I have. You can do the same thing here, if you give it a shot. I bet, among your people, you're used to being one of the strongest and most dominant, right? But here in Grizzly Cove, you can't make the same comparisons because you're not comparing apples to apples. You're an orange, my friend. Just like I was in my Clan. Just like I am here, in fact."

"I'm an *orange*?" His lips turned up at the corners, and his eyes twinkled at her.

She bumped into his shoulder with hers.

"You know what I mean." She chuckled with him, feeling a companionable mood settle over them. It was easy to talk to him. Like they'd been friends forever, and not just for an hour.

"Yeah, I do, and it's kind of you to attempt to give me a pep talk." They sat side by side, their shoulders touching, almost leaning on each other.

"Is it working?" She peered up at him, giving him the side-eye.

Seamus straightened up a bit. "You know? I think maybe it is. A bit." He tilted his head to meet her gaze. "You're right. Among my kind, I'm an Alpha. I was *the* Alpha before I went walkabout."

"Walkabout?" She squinted at him. "Isn't that some Australian Aboriginal thing?"

"Yup. My name might be Irish, but my ancestry features more than a few Aborigines. The story goes that when the first O'Leary was sent to Botany Bay, he must've had a bit of magic about him from old Ireland because he mated with a local shapeshifter named Alinta. There've been more than a few Alinta O'Learys over the years. The name means *flame* in my tribe's language, and it certainly fits my old auntie.

She's still a pip, even at her age." He smiled, no doubt remembering his family.

"She sounds great," Moira said quietly. "So you went traveling, and somehow, that's how you ended up here?"

"I was captured in the bush, in my furry form, stuck on a boat, and eventually, I ended up in Oregon in a private animal collection up in the mountains. Those bastards knew some of us might be shifters. I think they were hoping we all were, but they were clearly misled on a few of the animals in there with us. Near as I can figure, the rich folks in charge were paying through the nose for each new addition to their menagerie."

"How long were you held prisoner?" she dared to ask. She felt sympathy for the awful experience he'd been through.

Seamus rubbed one hand over his beard-stubbled chin. "Months? I'm not really sure. It all blurred together there for a bit. It was a long time. Longer than I've ever stayed furry in my entire life. But I couldn't change and give them the satisfaction. They wanted proof that shifters existed, and I wasn't going to be the one to spill the beans for the rest of the shifting world."

Moira put her arm around his broad shoulders, squeezing gently. "That's a brave thing you did."

"It wasn't just me," he mumbled, looking away. He gazed out over the cove, the sun kissing his skin.

Moved by the moment, Moira rested her head on his shoulder. She felt a kinship with this strange shifter unlike anything she'd ever felt before. She was drawn to him, almost against her better judgment. But there was something about him…

"You're a beautiful woman, Moira Kinkaid, with a beautiful soul," he said unexpectedly, turning his head as she looked up from her position on his shoulder. The moment stretched as their eyes met…and then…

Seamus O'Leary kissed her. Right there, sitting at the picnic table in full view of anyone who happened to glance their way, but she didn't care. All that mattered was this moment. This kiss. This man.

Something inside her snapped into place, as if it had been waiting for him—just for him—all her life. Something that she hadn't even known was wrong suddenly became right.

Seamus.

Sweet Mother of All. Seamus O'Leary was something special. In fact, he might just be…

No. It couldn't be. Not that easily. No way.

She couldn't have just found her mate. Not today. Not this way.

Not with a guy who smelled faintly of eucalyptus. A koala shifter, for heaven's sake! As if she wasn't enough of a misfit in her Clan already.

But as the kiss deepened, her mind whirled. Why *not* Seamus? He was a perfectly scrumptious man, and he made her toes curl with his tempting kisses. He was just as good as—no, *better* than—any selkie or lion shifter. Just let those assholes in her Clan say *anything* about him! She'd teach them a thing or two about respect. Just see if she didn't.

Moira threw her arms around Seamus's shoulders when he turned to take her into his arms. They were doing this. Right here on the beach. Necking like teenagers. The thought made her want to giggle, as did the effervescence that seemed to well up in her body. A tingle of awareness and excitement. Seamus did that to her. He made her come alive as never before.

Damn. He was a *great* kisser.

Seamus nearly lost his head. Kissing Moira was like holding starlight…riding a sunbeam…finding perfection. She was magic itself to his starved senses, and he wanted nothing more than to kiss her for the rest of his life.

But he couldn't. Guilt ate at him and wouldn't let him rest. And when he thought about her other half, the guilt turned into something darker. Something filled with grief and remorse.

Much as he wanted to, he couldn't keep kissing her like this. Not under false pretenses.

He broke away, finding it near impossible to let her go. But he had to. She had to know the truth before this went any further. Even if he lost her forever because of what had happened, it was only right that she know the truth about him. About what had happened.

Her expression was dazed at first, then went to confusion. He liked that she'd been so involved in the kiss that he'd managed to put that dreamy look on her face.

"Moira, you need to know something."

Confusion turned to concern on her expressive face.

"When I escaped the menagerie, I wasn't alone," he went on, needing to say this to her before he got in any deeper. "There was a lioness and a selkie boy. The three of us got out the same way, during a power outage when we knew the cameras were down. It must have been an arranged thing, though we had nothing to do with it. Someone hit the compound and gave us time to get out. The others went with whoever set up the raid, but the three of us went on our own, out a different exit. I'm not sure why the lioness and seal boy went their own way, but for my part, I didn't know anyone in this country. I had no idea if the people who were running the raid were the good guys or just another load of bad guys. I wanted out, and I wanted to make my way home on my own. Safer that way, I thought. I guess the lioness and the boy did too. They seemed to know each other."

"They might've been from my Clan," Moira offered, frowning now. "If they were, then they probably did know each other. They might've even been family to each other. Lions and seals sprout up in the same families from time to time. They could've been siblings or maybe even mother and son, but I don't recall hearing of anyone going missing. And you say they were held for months?"

"I was held for months. I'm not sure about them. I only started seeing them the last month or so of my imprisonment, so maybe they were relative newcomers. Or maybe they'd been housed elsewhere before that. I'm just not sure." He understood why she was questioning him, but he was still surprised by her response. He had expected anger…though he might still get that when he told her all of it.

"I wish I knew who they were," she said in a calm voice. "If it's okay with you, I'll call my cousin, the lion Alpha, and ask if he's heard anything. If some of our people are out there and need help, he'll find them." Seamus was impressed with Moira's confidence in her cousin's abilities. "Did they stick together after you got out?"

"That's just the thing…" He really wasn't looking forward to telling her this next part. He sucked it up and got to it. No sense stalling any longer. She had to know. "The lioness was hurt. She didn't shift to human form while we were escaping, but the boy had to change. His seal form couldn't go very fast on land. For my part, I'd shifted the moment I knew the cameras were dead. I was sick of being furry and eating leaves. The boy and I let the lioness out of her cage, and he ran to her. On the way out, I snagged some coveralls the workers had left hanging on pegs. The three of us went out a side door and headed for the fence." He took a deep breath, lost in the memory. "It was an easy climb for me, but the boy had difficulty. I helped him while the lioness leapt. That's when I saw the marks of some pretty serious injuries on her fur. She'd been cut for some reason. I don't know. Maybe our keepers were experimenting on her. I have no idea. She never shifted so we could talk. Maybe she couldn't at that point. All I know is, we hightailed it, the three of us, into the hills."

He paused for a moment. The next part was the hardest to tell, but he had to get it off his chest. Not even Big John knew this part.

"We ran through the night, but the lioness was in bad shape. I think they'd cut her recently, and she was still healing. She found a place in the undergrowth where she could hide, and the boy—he told me his name was Eamon—said she wanted to rest and for us to go on. He was able to understand her gestures, I guess, but I don't speak lion. Never seen one that close before in my life, in fact. They said goodbye to each other, and I could see tears in the boy's eyes. He didn't want to leave her any more than I did, but we really had no choice. She'd be able to hide in the hills in her animal form. I might've been able to hide and evade recapture too, but the boy had no chance as a seal. He had to get out of there as soon as possible." He scrubbed one hand over his face, dreading the next part of his story. "So Eamon and I left her and took off again. I had no real idea where we were. I figured out later that we weren't far from the town of Gresham, Oregon, but at that point, all I knew was that we were in a pine forest the likes of which I have never seen."

"Gresham isn't too far south of here," Moira observed, her expression thoughtful.

"I stayed in the wild for a long time after my escape. I lived off the land for the most part and only talked to other shifters that would cross my path on occasion. That's how I heard about this place—from a wolf I shared a campfire with one night out in the Cascade Mountains. The wolf told me the Alpha here had put the call out for bear shifters, and I was hoping I could find some help, even though I'm not really a bear. I was ready to give up living rough and see if I could find a way to get back home."

"What happened to the boy?" Moira asked.

Had she realized he'd been stalling? He didn't want to see her eyes fill with disappointment in him, but he had to tell her truth. He owed her that—especially since she might be Eamon's kin.

"We were hunted. The folks from the menagerie didn't want to let us go that easily. I managed to keep us both one step ahead of pursuit, but late one night, we came up against a cliff and Eamon…fell. He fell right off the cliff, right in front of my eyes, and there was nothing I could do to stop him."

Moira inhaled sharply. "Did he die?"

"I honestly don't know." Much to Seamus's horror and shame, he hadn't been able to search as thoroughly as he would have liked.

The hunters had been hot on his trail, and

although he'd tried hard to discover what had become of his young friend, he hadn't been able to find a single trace. Seamus shook his head, as if to banish the memory of that horrible night.

"Tell me what you recall," Moira said in a calm voice. She was taking this better than he deserved.

He might've let that boy fall to his death, and he hadn't been able to find out for certain. It was a shame he'd have to live with for the rest of his miserable life. Alphas were supposed to protect those who came under their care. He hadn't protected Eamon, and that sad fact would never sit well with Seamus's protective nature.

"It was dark, and there was the sound of rushing water far below."

"Water? Were you above the river?" She sounded hopeful.

Seamus nodded. "As near as I could figure out later, when I had a chance to look at a map, I reckon the Columbia River was below us that night. My only hope is that the boy survived the fall and made it into the river."

"He could swim out to the ocean from there," Moira agreed. "I bet that's just what he did. He could stay in seal form for as long as he had to, if he couldn't find a way to come ashore and reach out to the Clan for help. About how old was he?"

"Early teens, I think. Maybe thirteen or fourteen?" Seamus told her.

"Then, if he's from Clan Kinkaid—and there's a ninety-nine point nine percent chance that any selkie in the States is part of my Clan—he's probably old enough to have had survival training. It's something our Alpha introduced for all the youngsters, and it's proven very effective in limiting loss of young fools or those who just end up in unfortunate situations. I'd lay odds your young Eamon is all right. He'll probably turn up sooner or later, if he hasn't already. I'm more concerned about the lioness. Did you get her name, by any chance?"

"No, I didn't. Sorry. It all happened really fast. We left the lioness in the forest the day after we escaped, and Eamon fell that night. We were being pursued the entire time and didn't talk much for fear of being heard." Seamus was a bit dumbfounded by her reaction. "I can't believe you're so calm about this. It's been tearing me up for weeks. It's one of the reasons I've been drinking so hard—to forget that boy disappearing over the edge of oblivion. I have nightmares about it almost every night."

Moira patted his shoulder. "You're an Alpha. That's what Alphas do when they can't protect everyone." She gave him a tender smile. "Plus, with what you've been through, you're not quite thinking straight yet, but you'll get over this."

"I wish I had your confidence."

CHAPTER FOUR

"I really thought you'd hate me for losing the boy," Seamus went on after a long pause.

Moira just waited him out, sensing he needed to come to terms with the trauma he'd been through. It wasn't easy for an Alpha who had taken responsibility for someone's safety to get over failing in some way.

"I don't hate you, Seamus. Far from it. I think you were brave to flee that prison on your own and courageous to try to protect young Eamon when you didn't even know him. If it helps, a selkie's instincts are to seek the water. It could very well be that Eamon scented the water below and dove for it. If the situation was as tense as I suspect, he might not have been able to resist his seal's urgings. I bet he'll turn up—if he hasn't already—safe and sound." She patted his shoulder again. "In fact, I can check with the Clan. We try to keep track of our members, no matter how far-flung. I'll see if I can get news of the lioness and young Eamon for you…to set your mind at ease."

"I'm ashamed to admit, I'm almost afraid to find out what your Clan may or may not know," Seamus said in a low tone.

"Well, I leave it up to you, but for what it's worth, I think it's probably better to know one way or another. Kinkaid may have no information about either of them. Or my Clan might know all about what happened to them. Either way, it's probably better to have that information. And I have to report this. Somebody needs to be looking for them if they haven't surfaced on their own already. But I'll leave it up to you whether or not you want to hear anything I might learn."

Seamus paused, and she just sat with him, waiting for him to reach a decision. She wouldn't rush him, even though she really wanted to be on the phone *right now*, reporting the incident. Clan Kinkaid didn't leave its people in trouble if it could be helped. The lion Alpha would want to know what had happened so he could send help.

"All right," Seamus said at last, releasing his held breath and shaking his head. "I reckon I need to be an adult about this and not an ostrich, hiding his head in the sand…or the bottle, as the case may be. I've wallowed long enough. Let's do this."

Moira smiled at him, rising from the picnic bench to retrieve her cell phone. Within moments, she was dialing the familiar number that would lead straight to the Alpha of her Clan. She moved off to the side a bit, looking out over the water as she filled billionaire Alpha, Samson Kinkaid, in on what she had learned from Seamus. Then, she listened.

Seamus held his breath as he listened to Moira's side of the conversation. She summed up what he'd told her concisely and with no show of emotion, like a soldier giving a report. That thought struck him as odd at first, but then, he realized she was one of the lion king's operatives. She was probably very used to providing summaries for her Alpha. Seamus's respect for her grew even greater. She might be small of stature, but she was a force to be reckoned with, he was glad to learn.

As the conversation went on, and she finished her report, she fell silent, listening to what the man on the other end had to say. She was facing away from Seamus, but at one point, she spun on her heel, and a smile broke over her face as she met his gaze. Then, she said the words that took a heavy weight off his heart.

"So, Eamon's okay?" she asked the Alpha lion, her face bright with happy emotion. "That's great news," she replied after receiving what must have been confirmation from the voice on the phone. She nodded at Seamus then. "I'll tell him. He'll be relieved to hear Eamon made it to safety and that the hunt is already on for his sister. Thanks, Sam."

Relief flooded Seamus's system, and he didn't hear much of her conversation after that. He dropped his head into his hands and prayed a prayer of thanks to the Goddess for delivering that boy to the safety of his Clan. If Eamon was with his family, Seamus could finally rest easy about the boy's fate and stop blaming himself for letting the youngster fall off a cliff.

Seamus dimly heard Moira wrapping up the call, and then, she was there, next to him, patting him on the back. He stood, unable to contain his relief and freed himself from the picnic table. He turned and swept her into his arms. She went willingly as he lifted her and swung her around in pure, unfettered joy. Eamon was alive, and he was safe with his family. Thank the Mother of All!

"It's just like I thought," she said, breathless when Seamus put her down and reluctantly let her go. "He scented the water, and his instincts pushed him to dive over the edge. He couldn't help himself. He was too scared. He felt bad about leaving you up there on your own, Seamus, but he had a route of escape, and he took it. He turned seal and swam down the river to the ocean. He actually swam down the coast to California, to a beach town he and his sister had been living in with some shifter friends, and was able to connect with them. They helped him get in touch with the Alpha, and once he alerted Kinkaid to what had happened, the search began for his sister. They haven't found her yet, but the search only just started, and Sam is also looking into the menagerie and who might've been behind it. He won't let them get away with what they did. You can be sure of that."

This was better news than Seamus could have dared hope for. Samson Kinkaid was known around the world for his power and steadfastness. If he put the might of his Clan behind this, nothing and no one would stand in their way. Justice would be done, and the lioness—and all the others who were being held in that hellhole—would be rescued, if they were still alive. Seamus felt his heart lighten at the thought.

Alone, he hadn't been able to do much. Even as Alpha of his people, he'd only had connections in his homeland. He'd never been to America before, and he hadn't known anyone here. Finding sanctuary with the bears had been a desperate move on his part, but even here, he didn't yet know who to trust, or how much he could trust them. He'd been hiding in the bottle for a while now, trying to get past the traumatic events of the past months.

Seamus knew he was damaged emotionally. Being caged for so long and stuck in his animal form had been hard. It was probably one of the harshest things that had ever happened to him and he hadn't dealt with it well.

His beast half had been traumatized by the imprisonment and had been in hiding ever since. The only time it rose to the position it should occupy in his mind was when he was blind drunk. A shifter wasn't whole without the consciousness of his spirit animal riding alongside his human mind, working in tandem, sharing the same soul. But the koala had been broken by the confinement, and it wasn't really talking to Seamus's human half. Not the way it should. Only when his inhibitions were lowered by excessive alcohol could he coax the shy spirit out into the light. It was another reason he'd been drinking so much, and he very much feared his fractured psyche might never heal.

Having to abandon the lioness had put a major dent in his soul. And then, losing Eamon in such a horrific way—or at least *thinking* he'd lost the boy—hadn't helped. Not at all.

But now, he had hope. Eamon was safe, and the wealthiest Clan in the States was putting all their might behind finding the lioness. That was fantastic news, and it went a long way to beginning the repairs on Seamus's battered soul. For the first time since escaping, he thought maybe he'd be able to find some sort of balance again. Some kind of normality.

"Eamon surfaced the day I left Houston," Moira went on. "That's why I didn't hear of it. Kinkaid's already mobilized his people in the area, and he's calling in reinforcements from a shifter mercenary group we've used on occasion. All top men who are based in Wyoming. They're already in Oregon, tearing up the mountains. Kinkaid asked that you speak with one of them. You might be able to give them valuable information about where you were being held and those you may have observed while there."

"I'd be glad to talk to them," Seamus answered immediately. "Anything I can do to help find the rest of the captives and shut down the captors for good, I'll gladly do."

"Good." She gave him another one of those heart-melting smiles. She was good at those. "I have to talk to the bear Alpha and figure out logistics. I think a lot of the bears here worked with the guys from Wyoming when they were in the armed forces. They probably all know each other, which will help."

"Why is that?" Seamus wanted to know. He wasn't quite following her thinking.

"Oh. Kinkaid thought it would be better if you didn't go back to Oregon right now. He thought it would be safer for all concerned if you didn't mind staying here in Grizzly Cove until they caught those responsible for the menagerie. If you were targeted as a shifter, they probably know what you look like in human form, so your presence in Oregon could tip them off that they're being hunted."

"If they're still there," Seamus added. He didn't like being told what to do, but he saw the sense in what she was saying.

Moira nodded. "Yeah, there's a good chance they're long gone, but there's still the possibility they think they're safe enough in the woods. And they may have lower-level accomplices that are local to Gresham. Kinkaid wants to get everyone involved, from the janitor to the top dog. This kind of thing can't be allowed to go unpunished at any level."

Seamus liked the sound of that. "All right. I'll stay put for now, but we'll have to give full disclosure to Big John. He was kind enough to take me in, but I don't want to bring any more trouble to his town."

"Then let's go talk to him right now," she said, already beginning to clean up the trash from their lunch.

Clean up. Yeah, he needed to do that before he met with the Alpha. It was only the respectful thing to do.

"Listen, Moira, I uh… I need to grab a shower and a change before I seek out Big John. I'm sorry I didn't do it before, but I wasn't thinking straight." He shrugged, hoping she would understand.

She offered him a kind smile as she stilled for a moment. "It's all right. I understand." And heaven help him, she really did seem to understand. How had he been so blessed to have this amazing woman find him on the beach?

Seamus had written off the fact that his mother had always claimed he'd been born under a lucky star. He hadn't felt very lucky lately, that was for sure. Getting captured and imprisoned in a private zoo hadn't been lucky at all. Then again… It had brought him here. To this moment. And this woman.

Maybe his so-called luck—what he would classify as *bad* luck to this point—had been bringing him to better things. Maybe he'd had to go through all that shit just to come out on the other side and find himself in America, of all places, with a gorgeous woman named Moira Kinkaid. It was something to think about.

But he'd leave those deep thoughts for later. Right now, he had an appointment with a shower that must be kept before he could go any farther down his path to redemption.

*

Moira was appalled to learn that the bears had been making Seamus stay at the jail. As she walked with him down Main Street, heading for the sheriff's office, which was located adjacent to town hall, she felt her anger rise.

"No, really, Moira. It's okay. There aren't any hotels in town yet, and though a couple of the bears offered me a room, I didn't want to be in anybody else's space. I needed to be alone, so the jail cell suited me just fine," Seamus insisted as they walked.

"It's a *jail*, Seamus. Way to make a guy feel welcome in town. Let him sleep in a jail cell," she muttered, angry even if his words did make a certain bit of sense.

"They don't lock me in at night. In fact, Brody gave me the key to the cells and the office. I have the run of the place, and I help out when they need a hand in the office."

Seamus sounded like the eternal optimist to her. She couldn't believe he was so calm about going from one kind of prison to another.

"Doesn't it bring back bad memories?" she ventured to ask.

He looked at her as if she was speaking in tongues for a moment, then he seemed to understand. She couldn't believe he hadn't made the connection between his imprisonment and sleeping in a jail cell.

"It's nothing like that at all, Moira," he replied, his tone amused. "I actually like it, because it feels like my own space. My own territory. I may share it with the sheriff and his men from time to time, but I feel good there. I can come and go as I please in whatever form I choose to take, and the facilities are much nicer than anything I've had for the past few months. Oh, the guys will occasionally tease me, but it's all in good fun."

"Tease you how, exactly?" Moira wanted to know. She'd kill anyone who dared hurt Seamus, even with a practical joke.

"Mostly it's eucalyptus jokes. Brody offered me a cough drop the other day. Then, Zak got a few of those decorative stalks of eucalyptus that florists use sometimes, and he put them in a vase on the bedside table in my cell. I put tooth marks on every leaf and put them on his desk to find the next day." Seamus laughed aloud at that, and she started to relax just a tiny bit. It sounded like typical male bonding behavior, if what he said was the extent of it, but she'd still be watching those guys like a hawk.

"Wait, there's a bedside table in your cell?" That didn't really fit the image she had in her mind of what a jail cell would look like.

"Yeah. Double bed. Bedside table. Reading lamp. Shelf full of books. Satellite TV. Phone. Stocked mini fridge. Coffee maker. Attached bathroom with shaving gear and a medicine chest complete with first aid kit. It's more like a guest room than a cell, to be honest. I think they built it with shifters in mind. There's another cell that looks like something out of an old western in another part of the building. I think that one's there for tourists. Come on in. I'll show you." Seamus opened the front door to the sheriff's office and held it for her.

They'd arrived, and she hadn't even realized it. She'd been so incensed by the idea he'd been staying in a *cell* all this time that she'd lost track of their position. She was intrigued enough by his words that she wanted to see if what he described was as accommodating as it sounded.

She walked in and found the sheriff there in the main office, standing over a filing cabinet. He looked up when the door opened and smiled at them.

"G'day," Seamus said by way of greeting. "Have you met Moira Kinkaid yet?"

The sheriff shut the cabinet drawer and ambled over, a faint smile on his face. "Yes, I have. How are you today, ma'am?"

"Fine, thanks, Sheriff," she answered, reserving judgment about the man now that she knew he'd been keeping Seamus in a cell. She wanted to see this so-called cell first, before she made up her mind about the man, and the town.

"Look, Brody…" Seamus eyed the other man. "I'm not trying anything here, but

Moira got concerned when I told her I was staying at the jail. She wants to make sure you're not locking me up at night or something."

Brody looked surprised, and then, his brows drew together in concern. Good. Let them know they were on trial with her. She wasn't going to take anything in this town at face value. Not until she'd done her own investigation. She realized that she didn't mind that they knew she was investigating. In fact, so much the better. Moira adapted her style to each new situation Kinkaid presented her with. In this case, she decided, open honesty looked like the best course. She had a feeling both the bears, and she, would be much more comfortable this way.

It wasn't her usual style, to be sure, but this trip had been full of strange new experiences so far. She supposed that would continue—especially now that she'd run across the first koala shifter she'd ever met. She hadn't even really known there were any. Perhaps they were rare? Or maybe they just kept to themselves. She wasn't sure, but she had a feeling she'd be learning a lot more about them before this trip was done.

"Nell mentioned you two had met when I

spoke to her a few minutes ago," Brody told them. He smiled as he gestured for them to go ahead into the hallway that led to other parts of the building. "Good to see someone taking an interest in Seamus's welfare. Maybe it's time to sober up, son," Brody added as Seamus passed him, giving him a heavy pat on the back.

Rather than take offense, Seamus paused to look back at the grizzly shifter. "Might be," he agreed, then turned to escort her into the back portion of the building—where the cells were located.

He opened a door, and the first thing she saw was a traditional cell with bars. Seamus ushered her right past it.

"This is the one they set up for tourists. As long as I've been here, nobody's ever been in it. See how shiny everything still is? I doubt they've ever used it."

She noted the new construction look to everything as they passed the open cell. Seamus opened another door that led to what looked like a meeting area that had several doors leading out from it. He chose the nearest one and opened it.

"This is my bunk," he stated, standing back for her to peek in the door.

She was relieved to find the room exactly as he had described. A double bed—big enough for the giant shifters who lived in this town—and all the amenities Seamus had mentioned. It looked more like a hotel room or maybe an officer's billet than anything else. The door did have a pretty substantial lock on it, and the door itself was made of steel. It would hold a shifter—as long as the construction of the walls was as strong as it looked.

"We had this room put in special in case we ever needed to lock one of our own up for some reason. It'll hold a bear," Brody said from behind them. She hadn't heard him approach. She'd thought they'd left him behind out in the front office.

Seamus took a key on a ring out of his pocket and dangled it from his hand. "But they don't lock it. Like I said, I've got the run of the place."

"I know it sounds bad," Brody allowed when she turned to face him. "But when Seamus showed up, we didn't have a lot of choices on where to put him."

"Plus, you did arrest me at first," Seamus reminded the sheriff.

"It wasn't really arrest," Brody protested

with a smile. It was clear the two men liked and respected each other now, even if they hadn't started off on the best of terms. "It was more like protective custody."

"Who were you protecting?" Moira asked, curious. Had the sheriff really thought Seamus could be a danger to Nell or her sisters?

"Him, if I'm honest. Seamus's biggest enemy is himself, as far as I can see." The criticism was said in a friendly tone that made it easier to bear. At least, that's the way it seemed, judging by the expressions on the men's faces.

"Too true, mate. Too true," Seamus agreed, his Aussie accent coming on thick.

"Well, I'm glad to see your *cell* isn't as bad as I'd feared," Moira began. "Look, Sheriff, Seamus and I need to talk with Big John, if he's available. I've spoken to my Alpha after hearing Seamus's story. There are a few things we need to discuss."

Brody nodded. "I can set that up. How soon do you want to see him?"

"As soon as possible," Seamus answered. "Samson Kinkaid hired some folks we think are former colleagues of yours. Do you know a mercenary group out of Wyoming?"

"Moore's men?" Brody asked, frowning a bit. "Yeah, we know 'em. If they're involved, I'm certain John will make time to speak with you. Let me just give him a call." Brody stepped away and pulled out his cell phone.

CHAPTER FIVE

The fact that John agreed to come right over to the sheriff's office after Brody placed the call impressed Seamus. He'd heard Brody's side of the conversation, and he hadn't mentioned Moira's presence, which left Seamus to wonder if the Alpha bear had come out of real concern for Seamus, or because he'd somehow heard the representative of Clan Kinkaid was in on this. Either way, it was nice of Big John to drop everything and come to them instead of making them go to him. Other Alphas would have been much more *lordly* about it, Seamus was certain.

Seamus cringed at the fact that he hadn't had time to get in a quick shower, but he'd spent a few minutes in his bathroom changing into clothes that didn't reek while Brody entertained Moira with talk about his mate's bakery. Seamus would've liked to shave too, but there was simply no time. He settled for splashing himself with a bit of water in strategic places and putting on fresh clothing. It would have to do.

John greeted them with handshakes and concerned smiles, commandeering the meeting space just outside of the room Seamus had been living in for the past few weeks. There was a conference table and chairs there, and John invited them all to sit, including Brody in the gathering since the sheriff was his second-in-command.

"Now, what's all this about Moore's men?" John began once they were all seated.

Seamus wasn't sure where or how to begin, so he turned to Moira. She seemed more than happy to take the lead, and he was relieved. The grizzlies had a way of intimidating him, even though he'd befriended most of them in his time here. They weren't as scary as they seemed, but they were still apex predators, and Seamus was very much still a stranger in a strange land.

"Seamus told me about his imprisonment," Moira started off, going for the facts right away.

Seamus remembered her phone report to her Alpha and was glad she was there to boil everything down to the bare bones. She was good at it, so he sat back and let her do most of the talking. She rehashed the salient points of his story, telling the bears about the lioness and selkie boy. Seamus hadn't told anyone that part of his story until today, so this was news to the bears.

When Moira got to the part where she'd called Samson Kinkaid, the bears grew very still. Both Brody and John had been frowning fiercely, but when they heard the boy was all right, they seemed to rally.

"What about the woman?" Brody asked, butting in when Moira paused to take a breath.

"She hasn't made contact, so we don't yet know her fate. Sam mobilized all our people in the area, but we didn't have many, and most are sea-based and not much good in the mountains. That's where the mercenaries come in. He got in touch with Major Moore and hired a platoon of his SAR guys." Seamus knew that acronym. SAR stood for search and rescue. "They want to send someone here to talk to Seamus and get his story first-hand. Sam asked me to clear that through you, Alpha. He wouldn't send anyone into your territory without your express permission."

John nodded gravely. "I appreciate that. Samson Kinkaid has always been known as a stand-up guy and a good leader. I know most of Jesse Moore's men, so I'll contact him and see who he's got in mind to send. Leave it in my hands, Miss Kinkaid. I'll make sure our Seamus gets to give his information to the right people, and I personally pledge whatever help I can provide in the search for your lost lioness."

Our Seamus, John had said. The term hit Seamus right between the eyes. It sounded as if the bear Alpha was claiming Seamus for Grizzly Cove. He hadn't expected that. Not in a million years. With those simple words, the Alpha was accepting him as one of his own. Part of his Clan. Under his protection.

It both rankled and felt amazingly good. Big John was an easy man to follow. He'd earned the loyalty of so many usually-solitary bears because he was a strong, thoughtful, big-hearted, brilliant strategist and commander. While Seamus was used to leading his own kind, his soul wasn't shared with the kind of apex predator Big John carried. It was humbling to be thought of as worthy of the Alpha bear's protection, and Seamus wouldn't soon forget the honor those simple words had bestowed.

"I'll pass that along to Sam," Moira said, smiling softly at the big bear shifter. "I guess you realize by now that I'm not just a low-level Clan member sent to consult because of my familiarity with the leviathan. I'm actually Sam's cousin and one of his top operatives. I *was* sent to help, and I do have knowledge of the leviathan, but I was also tasked with keeping my eyes open and reporting back to Sam about your town. He's very interested in what you're doing up here." Seamus hadn't expected Moira to out herself like this, but one look at John's face told him the Alpha bear already knew, or had guessed, her true purpose.

"I'm glad to have honesty between us, Miss Kinkaid," John said quietly. "I had an inkling that's what you were doing here, but I figured the town and its people would stand or fall on their own merits in your eyes."

"So that's why you were so interested in where Seamus was bedding down," Brody said with a smile. "For a minute there, I thought you might be checking out his digs for other reasons." Brody laughed, but Seamus felt distinctly uncomfortable, and when he looked over at Moira, she was blushing.

"I just wanted to make sure you weren't holding him prisoner too. The first time was bad enough, don't you agree?" Moira brazened her way past the awkward moment, but John's eyebrow was raised in speculation when he met Seamus's eyes.

"Rest assured, we have no plans to imprison anyone," John reassured her. "And now that the mer are here, construction on guest housing is going double-time. They've been good enough to spend their nights in the cove for now, but we have to create a better option, and soon."

"I'm lucky you invited me to stay in your guest cottage then," Moira answered.

"Here's a little secret..." Brody leaned in and mock whispered. "John's so-called guest cottage was a garage-slash-workshop until the day before yesterday."

John squirmed in his seat a bit, which Seamus found hilarious. Moira joined in his laughter and the tense moment passed.

"Well, then. I'm doubly honored that you would go so far out of your way for me, Alpha," Moira said graciously after the laughter died down. "I would never have guessed it was a garage. It's really rather cozy."

"You can thank my mate for that. She did all the decorating. I just did as I was told." John held his hands up as if claiming innocence, but he was smiling all the same. The pleasure he felt when he talked about his mate was obvious for anyone to see.

*

As Moira got acquainted with the waters of the cove in her seal form later that afternoon, she reflected on everything that had happened since her morning walk along the shoreline. Stumbling upon Seamus had opened up a whole new world to her. She hadn't known there were koala shifters. She hadn't known about the bastards who had been hunting shifters and holding them prisoner for months. She hadn't known that meeting one man could change her life, and her mission, so drastically.

She'd gone from being an undercover agent to blurting out her mission to all and sundry. She'd never done that before. It was kind of...liberating. And a little scary.

Moira had always worked from the shadows, hiding her true purpose, position, and abilities. Being able to operate in the open here in Grizzly Cove was refreshing. She liked the respect the Alpha had given her—and Seamus. This bear Alpha was more like Sam than she'd realized.

In her work, she'd met many people in powerful positions. Almost universally, she was dismissed by the bad leaders as a mere secretary or clerk, unimportant and unimpressive. The good ones treated her with a bit more respect, but still dismissed her as a mere underling. The really great leaders treated her as they would treat anyone in their domain, with equanimity and fairness.

In her experience, such leaders were few and far between, but when she found one, Clan Kinkaid usually did business with them in one way or another. It might be a partnership in some venture or the providing of seed money for a new innovation. Clan Kinkaid, as a business enterprise, and Sam Kinkaid, in particular, liked to invest in good people with novel ideas. If that didn't fit as a description of Grizzly Cove, Moira didn't know what would. If she had anything to say about it—and she had quite a bit of quiet power in her Clan—Kinkaid would be investing with the bears in the not-too-distant future.

After the meeting had ended, John had agreed to call Major Moore and arrange for a meeting between one of his men and Seamus. He'd already been speaking on his cell phone as she watched him walk out of the sheriff's station and down the street toward his own office. Brody had gone back to his paperwork with the assurance to John that he'd be ready to help arrange the meeting when needed.

When she mentioned needing to get to work surveying the cove, Seamus had offered to show her the new boathouse where water-based shifters could enter and leave the waters of the cove without anyone seeing them from shore. He'd left her there with a bashful smile and a promise to see her soon, though they'd made no definite plans. That had been a bit of a downer, but in such a small town, she was pretty sure it wouldn't be difficult to run into Seamus again.

She knew for certain that she didn't want to finish her business and leave Grizzly Cove without spending more time with the sexy koala shifter. There was something about him that just drew her toward him, like iron shavings towards a magnet. His story was compelling, and her heart went out to him for what he'd been through, but more than that, she found him fascinating on a very basic level. As if they'd known each other in some other life.

Moira shook her head. Even in seal form, she wasn't much for mystical thinking. She might be a creature of magic, but past lives weren't something she'd ever contemplated before. It was utter nonsense…wasn't it?

Moira stuck close to the surface of the cove as she made her way toward the mouth that would lead to the ocean. She didn't want to interfere with any of the mer who were making the cove into a home. She especially didn't want to be seen as a threat to any of the young that had accompanied the pod out of the ocean and into the cove.

Such a move was unprecedented. Moira had met mer before, in her travel in the ocean, but mostly, they kept to themselves. They were friendly enough, but since they had gills and could stay underwater indefinitely and dive deeper than any seal, their paths didn't often cross. Still, they were allies, of a sort, united in trying to keep the oceans clean and safe for their people and especially their young.

As Moira headed toward the somewhat blurry line that separated the waters of the cove from the ocean proper, she saw a flash of scales below her. It was too large for any fish, and as it drew nearer, she realized it was a mermaid. The woman was in her full mer form, covered head to tail in scales that hid most of her attributes, but the long, flowing hair seemed to indicate it was female. A female warrior, if the trident in her hands and the multiple knives strapped to her arms were any indication.

She smiled, though, when she came face to face with Moira's seal form, showing teeth that were sharper than human. The mer were really fascinating. When they shifted, they retained their human shape and size but gained gills and the ability to breathe under water.

Moira supposed that shouldn't impress her as much as it did, seeing as how Moira herself went from human to animal. It just seemed…weird, for lack of a better word, that they should still keep their human shape, yet change so much.

When the mermaid pointed toward the surface with her trident, Moira understood that she wanted to surface. Probably so they could talk. Moira would have to shift to full human form to do that, but she didn't mind. She headed up to the surface, only a few feet above their heads, shifting as she went.

By the time she broke the surface, she was human. The mermaid was only seconds behind her, and when her head popped out of the water, the scales had receded to below her chin. The partial shift was impressive—another thing about the mer that was fascinating to Moira.

"Hi, I'm Janice. I didn't mean to interrupt your exploration, but you're coming awfully close to no man's land. The waters of the cove are safe, but the area just beyond the mouth of the cove is seriously dangerous. I'm part of a group that's been set to patrol the boundary to warn those who might not realize, and help those who accidentally stray too far."

"I'm Moira. Thanks for the warning," she said, glad to see the mer were on top of things out here. "I actually just came to get a feel for the demarcation zone and see what might be waiting on the other side, if I can. I don't plan to venture over the boundary," she told the warrior mermaid. "Can you see the leviathan or its minions from here?"

Janice nodded, frowning as she turned her head slightly toward the ocean. "Yeah, you can see them. The little ones mostly, not the big guy. The leviathan itself seems to stick to the ocean proper, unless there's some kind of attack going on." Janice turned back to face Moira. "You're the selkie from Clan Kinkaid, aren't you?"

Moira smiled. "Word travels fast, I see."

"Small town." Janice shrugged, then seemed to relax. "Actually, three of my friends are mated to bears now. Two of them were savaged by the leviathan. Grace washed up on shore, and the game warden bear found her and nursed her back to health. They live over there." Janice pointed toward a house just visible up the beach. "Then Jetty went to investigate what happened to Grace and met her bear, Drew. He's the one who brought us all here. That's one brave bear Jetty's got. But Sirena, our hunting party leader, was gravely injured, and she ended up mated to the town's doctor, a giant polar bear shifter named Sven."

"Sounds like you're all settling in here even more than I even imagined," Moira observed.

"Yeah, I like it. And I'm really happy for my friends, even if their matings did break up our hunting party. Still, it's good to see them so content." Janice smiled again. "We were told a selkie had arrived and to be on the lookout to make sure you were safe. It wouldn't do to bring the anger of Kinkaid down on us, or the bears. You've been given safe passage and any help you need."

"That's…" Moira groped for an adequate word through her surprise. "That's really nice of you. Thanks."

"Oh, and Nansee—she's our pod leader—wants to meet with you," Janice added.

"I'd be honored," Moira assured her.

Meeting with a pod leader was a big deal. Selkies probably knew more about mer than most other shifters, but the identities of pod leaders were kept secret among their own people. That this Nansee had brought her entire pod here and was willing to meet with Moira was something unique. Historic, even.

"I think the meeting is scheduled for tomorrow morning over breakfast," Janice went on as both women tread water.

"I'm supposed to be meeting with the *strega* witch sisters for breakfast tomorrow," Moira said apologetically.

But Janice nodded. "Yes, that's right. Nansee was invited too. She wants to check out the Kinkaid selkies we've heard so much about—even under the waves." Janice winked as she laughed, and Moira joined in.

Well, all right then. These people were far more astute than Moira would have credited. It seemed she hadn't really been flying under their radar at all. They'd already had their suspicions about her position in the Clan even before she'd gotten there.

Good. That meant they were as cautious as she was, and quick thinkers were always better to work with than dullards. This might be the beginning of a good relationship between Kinkaid and not one, but two up-and-coming shifter groups…who just happened to live in the same town.

Unprecedented and historic. Two truths that were going to keep coming around, Moira suspected, as long as she was dealing with the shifters of Grizzly Cove.

CHAPTER SIX

That Seamus was waiting for Moira in the boathouse when she came out of the water was a bit of a surprise, but a welcome one. He'd showered, changed again, and shaved.

Ooh la la, he cleaned up well. Seamus was even more handsome than she'd thought, and her knees went a little weak when she came out of the changing area and found him waiting in the gift shop area at the front of the building.

As she approached, he brought out a flower wrapped in cellophane from behind his back. A long-stemmed pink rose. A symbol of friendship and affection, if she remembered correctly. How sweet. Her heart melted a little when he held it out to her and gave her that crooked smile of his.

"For you, Moira. For not dumping me in the ocean, when you had the chance."

That was it. She was a goner.

Moira took the rose from his hands and smiled up at him. He was taller than her, though he wasn't as massive as the grizzly men in this town. Still, he was just the right size for her not to feel completely overwhelmed and bring on feelings of panic from her other half. He was perfect for her.

And where had *that* thought come from? Probably from the same wretched place that had her thinking of long-term commitments from a man she'd only just met. The same place that whispered what a good mate Seamus would make.

Yikes. She'd better be careful before she broke her own heart on a man who would no doubt be planning, even now, on returning to his own country and his own people. How would she—a seal shifter—fit in with a bunch of koalas?

And would he even ask her to try? She had no idea if he was feeling the same amazing things she was experiencing. Maybe this was all just a mild flirtation to him. Maybe he was just being nice because he was grateful she'd helped him and was understanding about the trauma he'd just been through. Maybe her inner seal was barking up the completely wrong tree.

"Thank you, Seamus." She took the flower and held it to her nose, enjoying the soft scent of rose. One of her favorites.

"I was wondering if you'd be my guest for dinner. Zak is very close to opening his restaurant, and he invited a few of us over tonight to try out some of the selections he's thinking of putting on the menu. It'll be a bit of a working dinner, since he'll be asking you for your opinion of each dish, but I can guarantee you'll enjoy it. He's one of the best chefs around. Do you like Cajun food?"

"Actually, I love it. And I'd love to accompany you. Thanks for asking."

A date? She was going out to dinner with sexy Seamus? Yes, please.

"Do you need to go back to the *guest cottage* to freshen up or anything?" he asked, emphasizing the two words with a twinkle in his eye. They both now knew her accommodations had been a garage until the day before yesterday.

"No, I used the showers here. They have all the amenities. Soaps, lotions, towels, even changes of clothing, if you need them. It's a water shifter's dream come true."

"We just built the place. The mer stocked it with what they wanted." Seamus shrugged as if it was no big deal, but to Moira, it really was remarkable what they'd done in such a short amount of time.

"Did you have a hand in building it?" Moira asked, picking up on his casual use of the word *we*.

Seamus shrugged again. "I have nothing else to do with my time and no consistent access to funds in this country. I have to do something to earn my keep, and I know carpentry. Put a hammer in my hands, and I'm handy enough. I also did the tile work in that shower area. Did you like the little swish patterns?"

"You mean that gorgeous mosaic of tiny tiles making a wave over the wall?" Now, she was truly impressed. "Seamus, that's a work of art. *You* did that?"

He looked a little embarrassed by her praise. "I like working with tile. I remodeled the kitchen and all the bathrooms in my mother's house a few years back. The patterns I designed for her were a bit more complex and took more time. Turned out well, I think. At least Mum seems to like them." They began walking toward the door to the street. "It's actually good that you don't have to go back to the cottage. Zak's invitation was for six, and it's almost that now. If we mosey over there, I reckon we'll get there right on time."

She allowed him the change in subject, since he seemed uncomfortable talking about his artistic accomplishments. Someday, though, she'd love to see what he could do with his mosaic designs given more time. The work he'd done on short notice in the boathouse was truly beautiful.

"Well, then. Shall we?"

Seamus felt like a king, walking with Moira at his side down the quiet Main Street in Grizzly Cove. He felt even better when they entered the newly constructed building that would be Zak's restaurant, as soon as they opened officially. Tonight, there were just a few people there, invited specially by Zak, to help him settle on the menu.

Big John and his mate, Urse, greeted them by the door, having apparently just arrived themselves. From there, they said hello to Sheriff Brody and his mate, Nell, her sister Tina, who was Zak's mate, and their other sister, Ashley and her mate Tom. Luckily, Moira had met them all before, so there was no need for Seamus to make the introductions. He was still relearning how to be human after spending so long in his fur, and sometimes, polite conversation was still a bit beyond him.

Another couple was already seated, but Tina introduced them. It was the town doctor, Sven, and his new mate, the mermaid, Sirena. Sven still insisted on checking Seamus out every week or so to see that he was gaining weight and recovering from his ordeal. He'd also talked to Seamus about his drinking, but the polar bear shifter had also been a soldier, and he understood post-traumatic stress and how shifters dealt with it.

Seamus knew, somewhere in the back of his mind, that Sven wouldn't have let Seamus go on with his drunken behavior indefinitely. Sooner or later, the polar bear would have intervened. Oddly enough, since that morning when Moira had walked into his life, Seamus hadn't even thought about drinking, and when the idea arose in his mind now, he felt no real interest.

He'd been drinking to get in touch with his inner animal and forget his guilt over losing Eamon that way, but the guilt had dissipated now that he knew Eamon had jumped rather than fallen by accident. And everything had turned out okay. Moira had put Seamus back in touch with his wild side. Eamon was safe. And Seamus's unnecessary guilt had lifted. With it, his need to drink to excess had dissipated. Funny how that worked. Grizzly Cove was going to soon realize that their town drunk had gone dry. He wondered what they'd make of that and knew they'd be happy he was finally getting his shit together.

The gathering in the unopened restaurant was cozy and loud, with multiple conversations going on at any given time as Zak and his mate brought out plate after plate of delicious-smelling food from the kitchen. Everybody got to try a little of everything and give their opinions before Zak took orders for whatever anybody wanted more of. Every dish was great as far as Seamus was concerned, so it was hard to make up his mind when asked what he wanted Zak to cook him for dinner.

"Well, which ones were your favorites?" Tina asked Seamus, trying to coax him into a decision.

"I'm not sure. Maybe the crab? Or the steak?" He really wasn't sure.

Tina patted his arm. "I'll bring you both," she assured him and went off to join her mate in the kitchen. Seamus wasn't sure he could eat that much, but she was gone before he could object.

"Smart man," Sven said, winking. "That's one way to get a double portion."

"I wasn't trying to do that. In fact, it'll probably be too much if she really brings both."

Sven frowned, and his voice dropped to a quieter level. "You lost a lot of weight, Seamus. You should eat it all, if you can."

"Honestly, I'm still recovering from all that eucalyptus they fed me in that menagerie. My human taste buds haven't come back all the way yet." Seamus hadn't ever admitted to that before, and he could see he'd surprised Sven.

Moira put her hand over his on the table for all to see. She was offering comfort. He hadn't realized she was listening to his conversation with the doctor just then, but he was glad of her support. She made him feel so much stronger, just by touching his hand.

"Didn't they give you anything else?" she asked softly.

A sort of hush fell over the group, and he realized they were all aware of the intensity of the conversation going on at his end of the big table. He didn't like the attention, but these were friends. He hadn't been totally honest with them, preferring to hide his troubles in a bottle, but the time for that was over. Moira—and the answers she'd provided—had changed everything. It was time to be more honest with these good people who had taken him in.

"You know, at first, eucalyptus is like ambrosia to my other form, but when I change back to human, it always leaves a funny taste in my mouth for a little while," he admitted, knowing everyone was listening, but not minding it so much. "Being stuck in my fur for so long made everything a bit harder this time. It's like I've had to learn to be human all over again."

The men around the table nodded or frowned, but all were supportive in their quiet acceptance of his words. Seamus could feel their silent encouragement, and it meant more than he could say. A clatter of dishes preceded Zak into the room.

"Man, you still smell like cough drops to me, and you've been here a long time," Zak said, slapping Seamus on the back on his way past, delivering more plates to the table.

Obviously, he'd been listening from the kitchen. Sharp shifter hearing had brought the words to him, even as he worked.

Laughter greeted Zak's teasing words, and the tense moment passed. The Cajun bear was good at defusing tension. It seemed to be his role in the Clan, more often than not, and Seamus was glad of his presence. He was turning into a really good friend, which was something Seamus hadn't expected. And it went almost without saying that he was one hell of a chef.

The rest of the dinner passed in discussion of the various dishes Zak prepared for everyone. The bears were honest in their appraisal of their friend's cooking talents, and Moira enjoyed their cheery banter. She also got a chance to speak with the women and realized that one and all were in the middle of an extended honeymoon period when love just shone in their eyes as they looked at their mates.

A different woman might have been jealous, but Moira was touched by the genuine emotion she saw between all the couples. She was happy for them and, okay, a bit envious. She wanted what they'd found. She wanted a mate of her own and the chance at lifelong happiness.

Which made her think about Seamus and the way it felt so natural to spend time with him. It was as if they were two halves of a longstanding partnership, even if they'd only known each other for a day. It was like finding a friend you hadn't known you'd lost and picking up right where you left off. He was easy to be with and easy to laugh with, even while working through the residual pain of his recent past.

She was glad she'd been able to give him closure on Eamon's fate. If fate allowed, she'd take him to meet Eamon at some future date, so he could see for himself that the boy was thriving. She could arrange that through her connections in the Clan. She thought it would be good for Seamus and his continued recovery.

When it came time to leave, Moira truly felt as if she'd made some new friends that night. The bears were a lot less scary than she thought they'd be, and their mates were amazing women. Even the Alpha female, the *strega* witch, Urse, had proven to be a down-to-earth modern woman who Moira could relate to. The fact that Urse had amazing magical powers didn't seem to faze her or her friends at all.

They were all, for lack of a better word, more *human* to her now after spending time dining and laughing with them as a group. Maybe that had been engineered, but at no time during the evening did she feel she was being manipulated. Perhaps, after all, it had been just a spur-of-the-moment invitation from Seamus to a party he'd already been invited to join. If so, the company couldn't have been more welcoming. They'd included her—a stranger to town—as if she were one of their own.

"I hope you'll allow me to walk you home," Seamus said with the gallant offer of his arm as they stood outside, saying goodbye to everyone. The night had gone on from dinner to dessert, to drinks, and the hour was late. Time had simply flown while in such amiable company.

"Why, yes, kind sir, I believe I'll take you up on that offer." She took his arm with a comical widening of her eyes as she leaned in, stage whispering so everyone could hear. "I understand there are bears in these woods."

"That there are, milady," Seamus confirmed, nodding wisely. "But I'll protect you."

"Yeah," Brody put in. "He'll scare them all away with his cough drop scent."

Everybody laughed, including Seamus, and they all moved off in mostly different directions. John and Urse walked with them toward their home, since Moira was staying in the small cottage on their grounds. They didn't seem to mind that Seamus was accompanying her. In fact, Urse gave her a wink as they parted at the base of the walkway that lead up to their house.

"Try not to keep her up too late, Seamus," Urse said, teasing them both. "She's got a breakfast meeting in the morning."

"I hear and obey, mighty Alpha," Seamus said, saluting her with that sexy crooked grin of his. Urse laughed and waved them off as the Alpha couple turned toward their home.

Seamus fell into step beside Moira as they headed around back on the secluded forest path that led to the former garage that was now a guest cottage. The place had all the amenities. A single room with a closet and bathroom along one wall, it was perfect for a weary traveler to lay her head. At least, Moira had been enjoying the little cabin in the woods since she'd arrived. It had been just perfect for her. Stoutly built with a good lock on the door, the cabin felt safe and Moira hadn't feared for her safety, even if she was in the middle of the woods where, she knew for a fact, many bears roamed.

There was a small fridge stocked with snacks and drinks, as well as a TV with satellite service and all the comforts of home. The bed was on one side, closer to the bathroom, and a sitting area dominated the other side of the small building. There was sofa and coffee table that currently held Moira's laptop and the files she'd been working on. There wasn't any truly sensitive data on the laptop, but she could access the Kinkaid databases from anywhere as long as she had secure wifi.

When they reached her door, Seamus

paused. Moira took a leap of faith and decided to invite him in.

"Do you want to come in for a nightcap? I have sodas and juice in the fridge. Nothing alcoholic, I'm afraid," she said, before she thought about how he might take her words. Luckily, he didn't seem to take offense.

"After the past few weeks, I think I've pickled my insides enough. Juice sounds good, thanks."

His crooked smile was enough to make her knees go weak. Especially in the dim light of the little solar lights that lit the path to the cottage doorway. She could see Urse's influence on the décor now that she knew the place had been constructed just for her visit.

Moira unlocked the door and led the way in, flipping on the switch by the door that illuminated a small table lamp in the corner by the TV. She thought about Seamus's words and the fact that she hadn't seen him drink a drop of alcohol at dinner, even though the wine and beer was flowing freely. Perhaps he hadn't had a drinking problem so much as a problem with not knowing what had happened to Eamon. Now that he knew, it really seemed like the need to drink had left him.

"Have a seat. I'll get the drinks," she invited as they walked into the cabin.

"I like the color scheme Urse chose. You'd never know this place was a garage two days ago," Seamus said, looking around as he sat on the couch.

"Did you help with the building here too?" she asked as she poured juice for them both and then brought it over to the coffee table.

"Nah, there wasn't really time. John did this one himself. There's a bit of a building boom going on in town, if you hadn't noticed," he said with a wink, leaning over to pick up his glass. "It's been all hands on deck ever since the mer arrived. Today was my first day off in two weeks."

She frowned. "Passing out on the beach at eleven in the morning is how you spend your days off?"

"It was either that or spend my time thinking too damn much about what might've happened to the kid," Seamus admitted. "I didn't even want the time off. I've been working as much as they'll let me, just to keep busy, but the materials didn't arrive on time, so everyone took today off to deal with housekeeping issues and whatnot. Generally, all you would've heard in town is the sound of saws and air compressors, but the supply shipment didn't arrive on time, so today was quiet, for a change. Tomorrow, we'll be back at it, I suspect. If the driver of that delivery truck doesn't get lost again."

"I can't believe I only just met you this morning. It seems like…" She didn't finish the thought, not wanting to sound foolish.

"Like we've known each other all our lives?" Seamus said in a low tone, saying the words she'd been thinking. Did he really feel the same?

"Something like that," she admitted, shy now that they were talking about important, personal things.

She had never been too comfortable discussing her feelings—or the feelings of the few men she'd been with in her life. It was easier just to enjoy the moments together without analyzing everything, but this time…with Seamus…everything was different.

"It's kind of crazy, isn't it?" She looked to him for confirmation.

Seamus moved closer to her on the sofa. She'd sat next to him after delivering the glasses to the coffee table, but she'd kept a respectable distance between them. A distance that was narrowing as they seemed to gravitate towards each other.

"It's the very best kind of crazy," he agreed. "And for the record, I'm feeling it too. It's not something I can explain or claim to have ever felt before. It's like everything's new and, yet, familiar in a comforting way. You calm my restless spirit, Moira. And you make me want things I probably shouldn't."

"I do?" she whispered as he slid ever closer.

Seamus nodded, holding her gaze as he put one arm along the back of the couch. They were both angled toward each other already, but he moved closer until their knees touched.

"You do, sweetheart. You pull me in like a raging river."

CHAPTER SEVEN

Moira was glad she was already sitting down when Seamus laid it on the line. His words made her knees tremble and her belly clench. The look in his eyes was serious as he moved slowly closer. He was going to kiss her, and she was going to let him.

No, not just let him. She was going to kiss him back. With interest. She'd been wanting to kiss him again since that first kiss at the picnic table on the beach. In truth, she'd been wanting to do more than just kiss him. She wanted to taste him—all over—and find out what it felt like to make love to him.

Never before had she been so instantly

and intensely attracted to a man. That he was a shifter unlike any she'd ever met before made her wonder if all koala shifters were this magnetic, but she dismissed the thought almost as soon as it formed. No other man could affect her like this. She just knew it.

Call it instinct. Call it fate. Whatever it was, she knew Seamus was, and always would be, unique in her experience. She wanted to know him intimately. She wanted to make love with him and carry that experience with her the rest of her life. Whether it would lead to some kind of future for them was still open for debate, but that didn't matter. What mattered most was right here, right now. This man, this attraction.

She moved into his arms and met him halfway. Their lips joined, and then, all serious thought fled as she gave over to sensation and the amazing feelings Seamus's kisses aroused in her body, her heart and her very soul.

When he advanced, she lay back on the couch, grateful it was a substantial piece of furniture, overstuffed and cushy enough to lay on without running out of room. It was probably built on grizzly bear scale, but was the perfect size for two more average-human-sized shifters like herself and Seamus.

What was even more perfect was the way he touched her, gently but with an urgency she felt too. She pushed at his shirt, wanting it gone, and he complied. Within moments, she was touching his skin. His warm, rough, hard-muscled skin.

He might have Irish ancestors, but the Aboriginal side of his family tree left him with a smooth creamed-coffee tone that was intensely arousing against her own much lighter shade of pale. She was freckled. His skin was tan, and the contrast made her want to move closer. Ever closer.

She clung to his muscular shoulders as they kissed, removing her hands only when she needed to so he could free her of her clothing. Before she knew it, they were both bare, straining against each other for the first time, skin to skin. The most basic form of communication.

She was completely nude, but he still had his pants on. It didn't seem fair. She wanted them gone. But just as she was about to protest, he began trailing kisses down her neck and onto her torso. He paused to lavish attention on her breasts, sucking and biting gently. Enough to tease, but not to hurt. Just the way she liked it.

When he moved lower, she gasped. Did he intend to…?

Oh, my. Yes. Yes, he did.

Seamus splayed her legs, supporting them with his strong hands, licking down the inside of one trembling thigh until he came to the spot that quivered in anticipation. And then, he was there. Stroking her clit with his skilled tongue. The wet warmth of his mouth made her pant as he explored her most intimate places with his tongue and lips.

When she could take no more, she moaned his name, coming against his tongue. She could feel him smiling against her sensitive skin as he kissed his way up her body a few moments later.

She was so lost in his kiss she didn't realize he was moving until her head spun. He had lifted her clear off the sofa and into his arms. She opened her eyes, only to shut them again as the world spun. He twirled her in his arms, almost dancing with her, until they were facing the direction of the bed, and she hoped to the Goddess that was his destination.

After that little taste of heaven, she wasn't

done with him. Not by a long shot.

"Where ya going?" Moira was proud that she'd been able to string three words together into a sentence. Her mind was still caught in the whirl of delicious sensation he'd caused.

Seamus placed her on the bed, then stood and backed away. For a moment, she was afraid he intended to leave, but he smiled down on her with that crooked grin that made her heart go pitter patter.

"No place without you, sweetheart," he promised.

She watched as he unbuttoned and unzipped his worn blue jeans. Was there ever a sexier garment worn by man? She thought not.

When he was revealed, she caught her breath. She didn't know much about his shifter half, but the human half was…perfect. Hard where a man should be, and sculpted by the hand of a master, he was a masterpiece of the male form, come to life. She felt womanly and sexy when his eyes flared as he watched her…waiting for him…ready for whatever he might have in store.

She beckoned to him, and he didn't wait a

moment longer. He strode forward, leaving his clothing behind him on the floor of the cabin, and joined her on the wide bed. She was especially glad the bears had opted for a large bed in the guest cabin. She hadn't expected to share it with anyone, but now that she'd met Seamus, she wanted to keep him with her—in her bed—for as long as he'd let her.

"Is it all right?" Seamus asked as he came down beside her.

"More than just all right," she told him, smiling at the man who would soon be her lover. "Make love to me, Seamus," she whispered, letting him know in no uncertain terms that she wanted him. She wouldn't give him any cause to question her willingness again.

"Your wish is my command, milady," he joked, dipping his head to kiss her playfully.

What started as something lighthearted and fun soon turned serious and sultry. One of his legs was between hers, and he stroked up her calf with his, widening her position while his hard-muscled thigh came close to rubbing against the spot that yearned for the pressure, the touch, the feel of him—any part of him. She was quickly becoming desperate.

The quick, hard climax he'd given her with his mouth had only set the stage for more. Her level of need rose quickly, making her grab onto his shoulders and practically demand that he fuck her. Right now!

She didn't have to say the words. He seemed to understand. Their bodies were talking on a physical level. She was rapidly approaching the point where words would become impossible as sensation took over with his skilled fingers playing with her breasts, his body caressing her in ways that made her squirm to get closer. He made her *yearn*. In a way she had never thought she could yearn for anything or anyone.

It was all new with Seamus. New and intense…and a little frightening, if she was being honest.

She wasn't afraid of *him*. Not at all. No, what alarmed her was the strength of emotion that making love with him caused to well up in her soul. It would only get deeper, she feared, as they came together, joining bodies and purposes, straining together toward a sweet oblivion from which she suspected there would be no going back. Once she knew what it was like to make love with Seamus, she worried she might be ruined for all other men…for all time.

But what a way to go…

She clutched at him, urging him silently to take her, to join with her and fuck her deep, hard, and without mercy. He seemed to get the message, thank the Goddess. Seamus moved over her, taking the place he'd prepared between her legs. One strong hand tested her readiness gently, caressing, rubbing and delving into the wet folds that were desperate for something harder, thicker, longer and much more satisfying.

And then, he gave it to her. Seamus joined his body to hers, taking possession with a strong forward thrust that was perfect in its timing, pressure and firmness. He took her over, overwhelmed her in the most pleasant possible way, and showed her things she hadn't known her body was capable of feeling…or doing.

He stroked within her—long, slow strokes at first, then beginning to vary in rhythm, thrust and motion. He brought her to a precipice, only to let her slide down again before bringing her to yet another high point. Time after time, he built the pleasure until she was certain she would go mad with it before he finished.

"Seamus! Please!" She begged him for relief, for fulfillment, for...something indefinable.

Then, and only then, did he relent. It was as if he'd been waiting for her signal to finally let loose his monumental control. All the finesse he'd demonstrated to this point was lost in a timeless moment of pure animal lust that swept her along with him into a maelstrom of sensation unlike anything she'd ever felt before.

Short, hard digs brought her to the highest point yet, and she screamed his name as she fell off the edge of the world, held safe in his arms, sliding into the most incredible ecstasy of her life. With Seamus. And only with Seamus.

He shouted her name as he joined her, and she held him, loving the tense quiver of his muscles as he strained in completion. She loved that she'd brought him to this point. She loved that he'd given of himself so freely. She loved the open, honest communication of their bodies.

Could it be that she loved *him* too?

Confusion clouded her mind for a moment, but the aftershocks of pleasure were still running up and down her nervous system. This was no time for deep thoughts. Right now, there was only time for bliss. Deep and delicious, utter bliss.

Seamus held her throughout the climax and its devastating aftermath. He was her safe harbor in the storm of sensation. When they had both caught their breath, he kept her close, shifting them on the bed so that he was on his back, his arm around her as she nestled into his side, her cheek resting over his heart. The reassuring thump-thump of his heartbeat made her drowsy, but how could she sleep when the earth had just moved?

"Damn, Seamus. That was pretty damn awesome," she whispered, needing to speak her mind to the man she felt closer to than any she had bedded before.

But how could that be? She'd only known him a handful of hours.

"I guess I don't need to ask, then, if it was good for you." He squeezed her shoulders, a simple sign of affection that meant the world to her in that moment. "In case you're wondering, you just blew my mind, sweetheart. I'm having a hard time forming coherent sentences."

"That good, huh?" She smiled, placing little kisses on his chest. "I think I like the sound of that." She levered herself over him and straddled his hips. Smiling at him, she felt his renewed interest against her thigh. "Shall we try something a little different for round two?"

"I'm at your disposal, Moira," he agreed with a wide grin and a devilish twinkle in his eye. "Do your worst, sweetheart."

She took him at his word, and this time, she fucked him, taking control of the situation from beginning to end. It was a heady feeling. None of her other lovers had ever let her lead the entire way. She could tell Seamus was holding back, letting her go at her pace, trying not to rush her, and she appreciated that he would give her that control.

Even if it was only just this one time, his patience showed her that he was a kind and considerate lover who gave as well as took. He was one in a million. Or perhaps, one of a kind.

He let her control their passion, and when they came, they came together, at her direction. It was a unique experience for her. Not one she would demand often, but it was good to know that Seamus was willing to give her whatever she wanted. Including himself and control over their shared intimacy.

That was more than most of the male shifters she'd been with were willing to allow, and it just pointed out to her again that Seamus was different in the important ways that mattered. With him, she could be herself and ask for control, and he'd actually give it to her, not just some facsimile of what she wanted, to be rescinded at whatever point he chose.

Maybe Aussie men were just more secure, or had more control. She wasn't sure if it was an Aussie thing, a koala-shifter thing, or just a Seamus thing. Quite possibly, it was Seamus who made all the difference, and she decided then and there to keep him around until she solved the mystery—at the very least.

Eventually, she slept, a great big sappy grin on her lips even as she faded into the oblivion of sleep with Seamus a warm presence at her side.

CHAPTER EIGHT

The next morning, one of Moore's mercenary shifters arrived by helicopter. There really wasn't any place to land in town, so the newcomer rappelled down a rope in a rather showy display of physical prowess. The chopper then flew off toward the south.

The commando show had taken place right in front of town hall, just as Moira and Seamus approached the bakery. He said he'd drop her off there for her breakfast with the ladies, and then, he'd go over to town hall for the meeting John had set up for him with a representative of Moore's mercenary group. The message had come through by text on Seamus's cell phone around midnight, along with a warning not to keep their guest up all night, so the Alpha definitely knew Seamus was still in the guest cabin with Moira.

She didn't know whether to be embarrassed or feel a bit triumphant. Shifters seldom gave a damn about things like nudity or others knowing who they were sleeping with, but Moira had spent her time passing as human more often than not, and some of their ways had rubbed off on her a bit. Still, she was among shifters now, and she saw no reason to hide that fact that she and Seamus had hit it off.

Certainly, they might have rushed to bed a bit quickly, as these things go, but everything felt so right with him she couldn't find it in herself to have any regrets…or embarrassment. The fact that the women of Grizzly Cove hadn't realized what a considerate man and great lover stood in their midst was to Moira's benefit. She had him now, and she was going to keep him for a good long while. The other girls were just out of luck when it came to the sexy Aussie.

That's where the triumphant feelings came in. She'd discovered his hidden talents, and she wasn't about to share him with anyone. He was hers for the duration.

"I guess that's the mercenary bloke," Seamus said with a grin, shaking his head as they looked at the man dressed all in black now heading into the town hall. The helicopter that had brought him was long gone, off like a shot heading back the way it had come as soon as the commando was clear.

"Maybe it's just a scout selling cookies," she offered, laughing with him as he snickered at her joke. She looked at the bakery just behind them and saw the ladies at the window. "Looks like my meeting is about to begin, and judging by that show, yours is too," she told him.

"Right you are," Seamus said, taking her into his arms and laying a kiss on her that curled her toes. "Think of me," he whispered as he let her go by slow degrees.

"After that kiss, how could I not?" she replied honestly, making him grin even wider. That devilish twinkle in his eye set her insides on fire with renewed need, but this was *not* the time. *Down, girl.*

"Then my work here is done." He let her go completely and tipped his imaginary hat to her and then to the ladies still watching them through the window. "I'll see you after?"

"You bet. I'll meet you at town hall if we finish first," she promised.

"And I'll come here if my meeting ends before yours."

She didn't want to let him go, but she knew they both had important things to do. They would be together again soon, and that would have to suffice for now.

Leaving Moira at the bakery sent a little pang of longing through Seamus's heart. Only a day together, and already, he missed her when she wasn't near. After last night, things were more serious than he would have thought.

He believed in his heart of hearts that she was *the one*. But what did he have to offer her besides his undying devotion and his battered heart? He was an Alpha, but not like the apex predators she was used to in her Clan. She was cousin to *the* Kinkaid Alpha, for heaven's sake, known the world over as *the lion king*, though use of that ancient title had cooled since the humans had released that cartoon movie. The sad fact was, Moira was powerful in her own right, and they were a terrible mismatch.

They didn't even live on the same continent. Although…they did have Irish heritage in common. Somewhere way back in their lineages, their people had come from the same little island in the North Atlantic. Ireland. That magical isle of fey and storytellers, music and blarney.

Was that enough to bond them for life? He just didn't know.

With more questions about his budding relationship with Moira than answers, he headed into the town hall. He followed the noise of men talking to the conference room and found the man from the helicopter sipping coffee with Brody and John. All three acknowledged him when Seamus walked into the room.

Judging by scent, the new guy was another grizzly bear. Fitting, really. Moore must've chosen to send a bear shifter because of the town's population, figuring the other bears here might take to the newcomer more readily if they had their animal sides in common. Watching the easy rapport between all of them standing by the coffee pot, Seamus suspected Moore had been correct.

"Seamus, come meet Trev," John said, gesturing for Seamus to join them. Brody was already pouring a fresh cup of coffee and handed it to Seamus as he approached. Considerate of him, really. Seamus thanked the sheriff with a nod as he accepted the brew. "Seamus O'Leary, this is Trevor Williams. He's one of Moore's guys now, but he served with my group from time to time back in the day."

The pieces fell into place suddenly. John and Brody weren't accepting the new guy just because he was a bear shifter. They accepted him this easily because he was someone they knew from their military days. They had a shared history as well as a shared animal spirit.

Trevor gripped Seamus's hand with the bone-crushing strength he'd come to expect from these big bear shifters. Seamus returned the gesture, having learned not to wince as his finger bones ground together. The guys meant nothing by it. It was just their way. Most of them didn't really hold back their bear strength when they were dealing with other male shifters. It was only with the women that they tempered their power.

After greetings were exchanged, coffee poured and pastries from the open bakery box snagged, they all sat around the conference table. Trevor ate a few bites of the honey bun he'd chosen—a favorite among the bears, Seamus had noticed—and gave Brody compliments to pass on to his mate about the food. It was clear the men had prior knowledge of each other, and Seamus was inclined to give Trevor the benefit of the doubt based on John and Brody's warm acceptance of him. He'd known both the Alpha and the sheriff long enough now to trust their judgment. If they vouched for the new guy, then he was okay with Seamus.

"How goes the search for the lioness?" John finally asked, once they were ready to get down to business.

In reply, Trevor removed a thick wad of paper from one of the cargo pockets on his black, military pants. He placed the paper on the table in front of him, then lifted out the largest stack—a folded map, which he began to unfold and lay out on the table.

The men all stood to get a better perspective on the map, including Seamus.

He recognized some of the features on the topographical drawing right away.

"This is where Eamon went over the cliff," Seamus said, pointing to a clearly marked cliff that jived with what he remembered of their path. "And this is the path we took." Seamus traced out the reverse path with his finger until he came to a spot he would never forget. "This is where we left her. Did you find any trace of her here?" He looked up at Trevor, hope building in his heart.

"We found some traces of her blood there, but either she's very good at erasing her prints or Mother Nature has diluted the trail with rain and weather over the intervening weeks." Trevor pointed to an area of woods that didn't look that much different from any other section, but Seamus thought he knew what the other man was going to say. "This is where we found the abandoned compound. Lots of evidence of animals being kept there, but the place is now empty."

"Who owns the land?" John asked, his eyes narrowing.

"Unknown. It's wrapped up in a lot of shell companies and red tape from what I hear. Samson Kinkaid himself is working on it, and if he can't find out, nobody can." Nods all around to that statement indicated the respect other shifters had for the lion Alpha, and his political and business ties. "On the pro side for the lioness, we don't think she was recaptured by whoever ran the compound. They cleared out too fast and were seen by locals hightailing their way off the mountain. They didn't have any animals with them, and she was too injured to shift, right?"

Everybody looked at Seamus, and he nodded. "She was cut up. Looked like they might be surgical scars of some kind, but I'm not sure. She couldn't shift, according to Eamon, and I had no reason to doubt his word."

"He reported the same when he finally got word to his Clan," Trevor replied. "She was too weak to shift. It was remarkable she made it as far as she did with you before she could go no farther. She must be quite a strong-willed woman." Trevor sounded as if he respected the unknown female, and Seamus understood why. The lioness had been a noble partner in their escape, and he'd admired her strength of will and heart.

"She was amazing," Seamus said quietly. "I think she got as far as she did because of Eamon. If it had just been her alone, she probably would've given up long before, considering how bad off she was, but she was determined to get Eamon to safety. I could see it in her eyes."

"That could very well be. Seems she's his older sister. Must be odd to have siblings with completely different animals," Trevor mused. "From what Eamon said, they were captured together while on a field trip for his school. He attends a human school, and his sister was along as a chaperone on a bus trip to the local zoo. How's that for irony?"

"How long were they missing?" Brody asked, frowning.

"Three months. We know the date they were abducted and from where, so that gives us the start date. We know the time period where the folks from the compound were leaving, but that was spread over several days. We don't know when the big jailbreak occurred with any exactness because the jailors could have stayed for days or even weeks before deciding they'd been too badly compromised. Eamon isn't much help because he stayed in his seal form for weeks before making it to an area on the coast where he knew he could find help. He didn't keep track of the days."

"Neither did I," Seamus admitted. "Though I know when I got here, at least, and I can say that was about two to three weeks after getting out of that hellhole."

"Well, that's more than we had before. It'll help us triangulate the time a little closer at least," Trevor said. "The reason we're so interested in the timing is that we have lion input from the Kinkaids on possible outcomes and timeframes for their female. For instance, they've given us an idea how much terrain she could cover if well or injured, which gives us parameters for a range to search. Unfortunately, it's a very big range."

"Distance times time," Brody muttered. "And it's been a long time. She could be pretty much anywhere by now."

"Not anywhere," Trevor corrected gently. "We know, for example, that she would probably stay away from population centers, so that helps us narrow things a bit. And there are geological barriers that would prove impossible for her to navigate, even if she was completely well."

"All right," John said, holding up one hand to stop the recitation. "Why don't we do what we promised the Kinkaid Alpha we'd do and let Seamus here give you his full account from beginning to end?"

Trevor nodded agreement. "That's what I'm here for."

What followed was two hours of testimony and cross examination. A court of law couldn't have done better, Seamus thought. He was limp as a wet noodle mentally by the time he'd told his tale and answered all of Trevor's very in-depth questions.

When they were finally finished, Seamus left the bears to their discussion of the military search operation. John and Brody understood that stuff better than Seamus, who had never been in the military. He was glad to have unburdened himself to someone who was actively doing something to find the lioness. Now, he felt, his load had been lightened.

He'd volunteered to go back to Oregon with Trevor, but the same reasoning against that still held. Seamus was known to the bad guys, and his presence might endanger the operation more than help it. No matter how much he wanted to be the one to find the lioness and bring her back to her family, he understood the reasons why he should stay away.

As he walked out of the conference room and back toward the main entrance of town hall, he heard female voices ahead of him. Moira. She was there, and she was talking with Urse. They must've finished their breakfast meeting long ago and come looking for him. Well, Moira had come for him. Urse was probably there for her mate, John, and keeping Moira company while they waited.

"Ah," Urse said, seeing him coming down the hall. "Here he is now."

Moira turned to meet his gaze, and Seamus almost stumbled.

She was so beautiful. So magical and alluring. And his.

She stood and came to him, meeting him halfway. The ladies had been sitting on a bench by the window, just adjacent to the front door of town hall. They were in the reception area that fed the hallway leading to the rest of the building—the offices and conference rooms, and the big meeting hall at the back.

"G'day, Mrs. Mayor," Seamus said to Urse after kissing Moira hello. He kept his arm around her shoulders as they walked back toward the bench. She felt so good next to him, her presence stabilizing and reenergizing him at the same time.

Urse laughed. "It's just Urse, Seamus. No need to apply my husband's title. He's the mayor, not me, and I'm very happy that way."

Seamus tipped his imaginary hat to her. "Right you are, ma'am." He squeezed Moira's shoulders. "Thanks for keeping my lady company. Your mate is talking military jargon with his visitor and Brody. I left them to it."

Urse rolled her eyes. "Great. That'll keep him occupied for another few hours if I don't remind him about the twenty million other things on his to-do list for today." She stood and headed toward the hallway. "Good to see you, Seamus."

Seamus and Moira said goodbye to Urse as she left for the conference room. Then, he turned Moira in his arms and gave her the steamy kiss he'd been craving since they parted that morning. It had been much too long since she'd been in his arms. He was greedy, dammit. He wanted all her time, though he knew that was impractical at best.

He'd have to settle for whatever moments they could steal from the day to be together. He was okay with that…as long as she was. He sent a silent prayer to the Goddess, hoping Moira would want to be with him far into the future. Maybe even…forever…

CHAPTER NINE

As far as Moira was concerned, the morning had been a great success. She'd met Nansee, the mer pod leader, and liked the woman very much. They'd discussed the leviathan problem in detail while Mellie and Urse asked questions and added their own magical observations. It turned out that Moira had much more in common with the mer than she'd thought, and Nansee had admitted to the same. She'd even extended an invitation to swim freely in the cove, even among the newly claimed homestead areas the mer had been industriously building.

As a selkie, Moira could dive, but she

couldn't stay below water as long as the mer. Still, the offer of safe passage and welcome among her people that Nansee had extended was something Moira hadn't expected. In return, Moira had told Nansee that the Kinkaid Alpha was interested in opening a dialogue between the mer and the selkie part of the Kinkaid Clan. This was the first step in diplomacy, and frankly, Moira hadn't thought she'd get any further than making the offer. Instead, not only was the offer accepted, but the mer had extended the hand of friendship.

Moira would be careful, of course. She was wary by nature. But she had a feeling that this was the start of something big. A beginning of cooperation among the sea shifters that hadn't existed in a very long time…if ever. There were stories, of course, of the sea-based shifters working together to fight the Destroyer of Worlds. If the worst should come to pass and that fiend had truly reentered the mortal realm, then perhaps the need for all creatures who served the Light to present a united front would also return. If so, they were laying the groundwork now.

If not, it was still a good move to be on friendly relations with the other creatures of the sea—especially a powerfully magical group like the mer. Nansee hadn't been able to speak for any pod except her own, but she was in contact with other pod leaders and would send the message to them that the Kinkaid Alpha was interested in forming alliances. Whether or not the others would respond, Nansee had warned, was up to them, but Moira was hopeful for good results.

"How did your meeting go?" Seamus asked her as they left the town hall.

"Very well. I really like Nansee, and we were able to pool our knowledge of the creature. I think it'll help Mellie in her potion-making, at least. Urse is going to present a detailed summary to her mate."

"Sounds like you made good progress." Seamus kept his arm around her as they walked down the street, and she loved the way it made her feel protected and…sort of…cherished. Such gestures from men had been few and far between in her life. "We did too, though I felt really wrung out at the end of that grilling I just took."

She touched his hand and turned her head to look up at him. "Are you okay?"

"Right as rain. Or, I will be, once I've had

something more substantial than just pastries to eat, and a chance to be around you for a bit. You steady me, Moira. I never thought I'd say something like that, but the minute I saw you sitting there, waiting on the bench, I started to feel better." He leaned down and kissed her, right there on Main Street. A good toe-curling kiss that set her to thinking of ways to get him alone as soon as possible.

"What are you doing for the rest of the day?" Moira asked him when he finally let her up for air. He must've seen the invitation in her eyes because his expression instantly filled with regret.

"I promised Lyn Ling I'd go over to her shop and finish the tile mosaic she asked me to do there. I already did one in the ladies room and one in the gents, but she wanted a piece in the small vestibule leading to them to tie it all together. It should only take a couple of hours to finish up, and she wanted it done in time for the weekend, so I really should get to it today."

"That's okay," Moira told him. "I should go for another look around the cove myself. Nansee was very welcoming, and I'd like to firm up those new bonds of friendship and cooperation with some of her people. Janice will probably accompany me on another tour of the perimeter if I ask her." She started thinking about how her afternoon would shape up. "Is it too early for lunch? You mentioned getting some more substantial food."

"Yeah, I could go for lunch, if you're up to it, that is. If you want to wait, I can too. It's your call," Seamus told her gallantly.

They ate lunch together, repeating what they'd done that first day—only twenty-four hours ago, when they'd met. This time, though, Seamus went into the bakery and made nice with the sisters, only two of whom were there today. They were gracious and welcomed him, assembling sandwiches that were even larger than their usual massive creations.

Seamus and Moira ate their meal at the same picnic table, but the mood today was so much lighter, so much happier. They touched often, holding hands across the table when they weren't needed to hold their sandwiches. They smiled a lot and generally enjoyed each other's company.

All too soon, the food was consumed, and it was time to get on with their days. Seamus escorted her to the boathouse, from which she'd make her entrance to the water. Janice was there already, waiting for her. Seamus left Moira with a hot kiss that kept her warm for long minutes while Janice teased her about her fondness for the koala shifter.

"Nansee sent the word down that you're to be given every welcome," Janice told her as they were stowing their clothing in lockers provided exactly for that use. The mer had really thought of everything when they'd set up the boathouse.

"Why do I suspect you had a lot to do with that?" Moira said, teasing her new friend.

"Well, she did ask my opinion, and I had a good time swimming with you yesterday. I can tell a lot about a being by the way they swim." Janice gave her a knowing look as Moira burst out laughing.

They laughed most of the way down to the water too, but then, they both shifted—Janice into her fishy mermaid form and Moira into her seal. Play was second nature to her seal form, and when Janice escorted Moira through parts of the cove that had been set aside for mer settlement, Moira found herself surrounded by a few curious youngsters. The pint-sized mer girls and boys seemed to enjoy playing with her, and Moira did a few tricks for them, but Janice put an end to the fun after a while, reminding Moira that there was a serious side to their swim today.

They went out toward the mouth of the cove, leaving the children and the peaceful parts of the cove behind. Even on the good side of the magical ward Urse had cast, Moira could feel the malevolent attention of the leviathan's evil minions. No one quite understood how the smaller creatures had tagged along with the big one when it had skipped through the numerous planes of existence and popped out in the mortal realm. Perhaps, the smaller creatures were its children. Or perhaps, they were a smaller variety of sea monster that fed off the leviathan's leavings. Either way, they were a problem.

She noted the way they swam—almost like a patrol—just beyond the influence of the magical ward. It was as if they were waiting for anyone foolish enough to step beyond the ward. Maybe this was just some sort of show of might. Some non-verbal way for the creatures to show the mortals that they were in charge. After all, they were effectively barring the only entrance or exit.

It wasn't effective because the mer were creatures that could live on both the land and in the sea, but Moira had no idea if the creatures understood such subtleties. No one could say for certain whether the smaller creatures had any sort of real intelligence. It was hypothesized that the leviathan was the brains, and the smaller minions just followed where it led.

One thing they'd been able to establish was that the smaller creatures did indeed follow where the big one went. Moira's Clan had done its best to track the leviathan while it had been in the Atlantic Ocean, and they were almost one hundred percent certain that the smaller creatures didn't stick around once the big kahuna left. They traveled as a group. A big evil, magic-sucking group of nastiness.

Janice helped Moira get a better look at the smaller creatures, and she noted the different look of the monsters they saw today versus the ones that had been patrolling the edge of the ward yesterday. She would ask Janice when they surfaced and shifted shape if that was the norm, and she would request through Nansee that the mer who patrolled this side of the ward begin to take notes on their observations—if they weren't doing that already.

Between the information Moira's Clan had already gathered and the things the mer could see from this unique vantage point, they might just be able to come up with some solid intel on the creatures and their leader. Moira wasn't sure what it would mean in the grand scheme of things, but she'd always believed that knowledge was power. The more they knew about the enemy, the more likely they'd learn something that would help them combat it in the long run. And this set up was the perfect place to observe the creatures from a position of relative safety. It would be foolish not to take advantage of it.

Moira spent a valuable few hours with Janice, but eventually, it was time to head back to land…and the scrumptious man who waited for her there. With Seamus to go back to, Moira was feeling less and less like spending all her free time in the water, no matter how inviting Grizzly Cove was to her seal side.

*

Seamus spent his afternoon working with tile. It was a hobby that could easily become an obsession for him. He had dabbled in tile mosaics before, but here in Grizzly Cove, he had been able to immerse himself almost completely in the work…the art. He'd been able to forget his troubles—if only for a short time—by working with the tiny shapes and bright colors. He'd discovered an art form that spoke to some heretofore unknown part of his psyche.

Lyn Ling was a recent immigrant from mainland China. She'd come to Grizzly Cove to make a new start after her mate had been killed. She was a giant panda shifter, and she had a young daughter named Daisy who was cute as a button in both her forms. Daisy had quickly stolen everyone's heart in the cove, including Seamus's.

Lyn ran a gallery on Main Street where she sold all sorts of bamboo sculptural pieces from wind chimes to garden fountains, and everything in between. It made sense, really, since both she and her daughter enjoyed bamboo when they were in their animal form. The first thing Lyn had done when she'd moved into the little house up in the woods that John and the rest of the bears had helped build for her was plant a stand of bamboo.

The gallery had an enclosed courtyard in back with a high privacy fence designed as a play area for Daisy while Lyn was working. The fence was lined with bamboo plants so Daisy would always have her favorite snack available if she went furry.

Daisy was out there now, in fact, playing while Seamus worked on his tile mosaic and Lyn rearranged the pieces in her gallery. Lyn's shop was the first gallery that had been completed, but there were several others on Main Street. They were all part of the cover story that Grizzly Cove was just some new artists' colony where a bunch of malcontent hermit artists had gone to get away from the world and create. When the tourist traffic increased, the galleries and public mission statement of the community would provide a reason for the town's existence, and also be a way to keep the place exclusive to shifters—or those they chose to live among them.

Seamus was happy while he worked on the mosaic. This one was an add-on to the already finished building. When Lyn had seen what he'd done on the boathouse, she'd commissioned him to do a few pieces to dress up her store. Seamus had been both flattered and happy to give Lyn some happiness in her life.

He'd known females who had lost their mates, and right now, Lyn was a sad, sad lady. The only thing that really kept her going was her daughter—a bright ray of sunshine in a gloomy world Lyn had to inhabit without a large piece of her heart. At least, that's the way Seamus had heard such loss described.

The Alpha part of his soul wanted to help those in need. Lyn and her daughter were females in pain, and the entire town had rallied around them in subtle ways, helping them get through the toughest times and try to forge a future. The mosaic Seamus was doing for Lyn was designed to make her smile. It contained protective glyphs from his Aboriginal heritage and was much more detailed than anything he'd done in Grizzly Cove to this point. He hoped it would bring Lyn some small bit of pleasure every time she saw it.

The complex work absorbed all his concentration, though a little corner of his mind remembered that, when he finished with this task, he'd be meeting up with Moira, and that made him happy too. My, how his life had changed in just a day. Moira had brought him closure on what had happened to Eamon and hope that the lioness was being actively searched for up in those mountains. He felt so much better just knowing those two facts, but Moira had also brought him hope for the future, which was something he hadn't had in a long time.

He worked steadily through the afternoon, and a few hours after he arrived, he finally finished the grout work. The mosaic was done. The design was set and would have to dry, then he'd come back and seal the grout in a day or two, but essentially, it was finished.

Seamus cleaned up, collecting his tools and sweeping the area free of any debris from his work. He was really proud of this piece and couldn't wait to see what Lyn thought of it. When he had made the area as spiffy as possible, he set his tool bag aside and went to find Lyn.

She was looking out the back door at her baby girl, smiling softly. It was a tender moment, and though Seamus hated to interrupt, she evidently heard his approach. Lyn's face turned to him, and she smiled faintly. She was such a brave woman, putting her all into forging a new life in a new country for herself and her little girl. Seamus admired her gumption. There was a wisdom in Lyn's eyes that was hard-earned.

"Is it done?" she asked, her voice heavily accented. English was most definitely her second language, but she was quickly gaining fluency the longer she lived in the cove.

"It is. Would you like to come see it?" Seamus felt like a conjurer about to pull a rabbit from his proverbial hat.

Lyn's smiled widened. "You bet." The level of enthusiasm in her voice made him feel a sort of joyful anticipation. He hoped she liked what he'd done for her.

He let her precede him back into the shop and followed slightly behind as she rushed over to inspect his work. She pulled the canvas cloth he'd put over the tile installation away in a rush, only to stop short, her mouth forming an O of delighted surprise, if he was any judge. Just what he'd hoped for.

"Seamus! This is beautiful!" She gasped and clutched the fabric to her chest as a tear formed in her eye. "Your soul is in this," she whispered. "A generous gift of art to my household." She turned to face him and bowed her head. "You honor me. Thank you."

Then, she went from formal to informal and rushed forward to hug him. She was a petite lady with the strength of a giant panda. Her hug was a little on the bone-crushing side, but Seamus was okay with it. He'd made this sad widow happy, and that helped heal his own heart a little bit.

She let him go just as quickly and beckoned him to follow her to the back of the shop. "Come. I have something for you now," she told him as they walked rapidly back to the door leading to the enclosed courtyard that was private for Daisy and her mother—and special invited guests.

Seamus had seen the bamboo-lined area through the doorway before, but he'd never been invited into the space before now. He felt honored. And he was completely floored when he caught a scent he recognized as he walked through into the secure space.

Sure enough, Lyn had somehow procured a gift that was perfect for someone like him. She bowed slightly as she presented a large potted plant to him.

"From your homeland," she said. "For your beast."

Seamus accepted the gift and damn if he didn't feel a bit of moisture gather behind his own eyes. He bowed to Lyn, trying to put into words how much her gift meant to him.

"You are a thoughtful and kind woman, Lyn. Thank you." He held the plant's fragrant leaves up to his nose and inhaled deeply.

For the first time since those amazing moments with Moira, his beast side stirred without needing the haze of alcohol, wanting to come out into the light. Seamus had feared, after being stuck in his fur for so long, the poor bastard was exhausted and didn't want to come out to play anymore. His animal spirit had been broken—or so he'd thought. Lyn's gift of a eucalyptus sapling was more than just a thoughtful gift. It was a token of hope.

It was Seamus's turn to pull Lyn in for a quick hug. She was such a sweet woman, this poor widow. She had a gentle heart that had been very obviously broken by the untimely passing of her mate, but she'd survived and carried on, and now, she was even showing signs of starting to live and enjoy life—at least a little—again.

A small furry body attacked Seamus's legs as he let Lyn go. It was Daisy, of course, in her adorable baby panda form, wanting attention. He put the plant down and picked her up, giving her a hug too. He met Lyn's eyes over Daisy's furry head.

"You've given me more than you know, my friend," he told her.

"As have you. Your heart is in your tile art, Seamus." Her simple words struck a chord in his soul. "If you stay here, I want you to do mosaic pieces for me to sell in the gallery. I bet you could make lots of money with them."

"I never really considered that, but it's a good idea. If I stay," he added. "I'll definitely think some more about it."

Daisy squirmed, so he let her down to play in the grass. She sniffed at the eucalyptus sapling, but it made her sneeze. Both Lyn and Seamus laughed as the little panda bowled herself over, then rolled around and headed for the plants she knew much better. In moments, she was nibbling on bamboo, and all was right with her world once again.

CHAPTER TEN

"The plant awakened my beast half without the need for alcohol," Seamus told Moira later that night, after they'd returned to her guest cottage. "I never said this to the bears, but I was really worried that my other half had been too traumatized by the imprisonment. I didn't think he'd come out for a long, long time…if ever. The only time I could sense him was when I was drunk. And after all those months in my furry form, I was heartily sick of eucalyptus, but the smell of my other side's favorite treat didn't turn either of us off. Instead, it made him stand up and make himself known for the first time—without me being drunk—since…"

"Since you escaped," Moira completed the painful thought for him. She took his hand, squeezing it. "I'm so happy for you. I can't imagine what it must feel like to not be in touch with your wild side all the time."

"It's not fun, I can tell you that," he whispered in a ragged voice. "I'm just glad it doesn't seem to be a permanent condition now."

"Well, have you shifted yet? The plant Lyn gave you looks intact. Didn't you even take a nibble?" she teased a bit, hoping to lighten the mood.

"To tell you the truth, I've been sort of apprehensive about shifting," he admitted, breaking her heart a little. "I haven't done it since that ill-advised drunken appearance in the bakery when I first got to town. And that was the only time I've shifted since fleeing the menagerie."

"All right, then," she told him, standing. "I think you should just do it now and get it out of the way. End any concerns you might have once and for all."

"You think it's that simple?" He looked so hopeful she had to bend down and give him a kiss. Before it could escalate, she made herself pull back.

"This doesn't have to be hard. I'm right here. I'll watch over you, and if you have problems, I'm here to help in whatever way you need." She tried to be reassuring.

"I'm not sure."

She squeezed his shoulders. "I am. Change now before you spend so much time thinking about it that you think yourself into a corner."

Seamus shook his head and smiled in that loveable, crooked way he had. Her heart melted every time he did that.

"You're right." He stood back and began unbuttoning his shirt.

Moira gave him a wolf whistle, hoping to keep the mood as playful as she could. She'd never seen a koala shifter. Heck, she'd never seen a koala up close. She was looking forward to seeing what Seamus's furry side looked like, and more than that, she wanted this…for him. She knew how it was to have two sides living in harmony in one body. Every shifter did. She sensed that Seamus had been a little lost since escaping because his beast side had gone deep within, traumatized by what it had been through.

Seamus needed the beast side to come back to parity within his soul. He wouldn't be complete until it did.

At least, that was her theory. She thought she was right, but the next few minutes should go a long way toward either proving or disproving her ideas.

Seamus grinned at her and tossed his shirt toward her, like a mini strip-tease. She caught it and gave him a comical leer when his hands went to the button of his jeans. *Hubba hubba.*

"You know, you could make a fortune in dollar bills if Grizzly Cove ever opened a strip club."

Her observation made him stumble and laugh out loud, which was just what she wanted. The mood was light and easy, all the better for his first shift since being held captive for so long.

His pants dropped to the floor, along with his kicked off shoes, and then, he was naked. He took a deep breath, and a swirl of gray mist seemed to envelop him momentarily. A few seconds later, he dropped to all fours, a lot shorter than he had been in human form. He was definitely smaller in his fur than he had been in his skin. Although…he was a bit bigger than she was as a seal, which she supposed meant he was a giant among koalas.

She approached him cautiously, taking the sapling Lyn had given him with her. She set it down in front of him before reaching out one hand to see if he'd allow her to touch him.

She shouldn't have worried. He accepted her touch and even seemed to bask in it when she scratched behind his tufted ears. He was so soft. And utterly adorable.

Then, he yawned, and she got a look at some serious chompers. Maybe koalas weren't as soft and fuzzy as she'd thought. They had some really scary teeth!

"I like this side of you, Seamus. Soft and cuddly, but with big sharp teeth." She chuckled as he began to nibble on the eucalyptus. "I'm so happy you found your beast side again. I want you to be whole."

Damn if she wasn't sniffling. It was just so beautiful, the way Seamus had been able to recover not only his dignity and pride, but also his animal half. She didn't know how long they sat there, on the floor of the guest cottage—him chewing on the plant and her watching him with a bit of awe and a whole lot of soft-hearted happiness.

When he finally changed back to his human form, he didn't kiss her lips, but he brought his lips to her skin, leaving a trail of intense sensation wherever he went. The eucalyptus must have left a little trace even when he shifted so that she could feel its exciting effects against her bare skin.

There were no words. Not at first. There was just feeling as he touched her and placed kisses all over her body as he undressed her. She was a willing participant, helping him remove her clothing so they could be skin to skin as soon as possible.

"That tingles," she whispered as he licked his tongue over a particularly sensitive bit of her flesh. Seamus chuckled, and she found the sound sexier than just about anything she'd ever heard before.

"That's the idea, sweetheart." He turned them so that she was on her hands and knees, ass up in the air. The animal spirit seemed to be riding him hard at the moment, but she was right there with him, feeling the same things. She wanted it hard and fast…and from behind.

"Come into me now, Seamus," she pleaded, not really recognizing her own voice. She was panting with need, brought on by the combination of Seamus and his talented, knowing tongue.

That seemed to be all the encouragement he needed as he positioned himself behind her and thrust home. She moaned his name as he filled her, loving the feel of him inside her…where he belonged. Two hearts beat as one as he began a slow, steady rhythm that soon escalated into something more savage. More primal. More exciting than anything she'd ever experienced before.

They were communicating on two levels. While their human bodies made love, their animal spirits found common ground in the passion they shared. Somehow. It was a tingling of magic she first equated with the residual effects of Seamus's kisses, but as their ardor escalated, Moira thought she recognized the electric zaps of her shifter soul rubbing against Seamus's.

She knew, from the lore of her Clan, that such things could, and often did, happen when mates joined body and soul. Particularly mates whose animal halves were not of the same species like the lions and selkies in her Clan…or the koala shifter currently teaching her things about her body and capacity for pleasure she never would have guessed.

Moira screamed as she came, then came again. On the third climax, Seamus mercifully came with her, stretching out the bliss that overtook her limbs, and caused her to nearly collapse in a heap. A happy little satisfied smiling heap. But Seamus was there to catch her. He supported her with his muscular arms, eventually lifting her up and taking her to the bed.

He placed her gently on the soft sheets, climbing in beside her and wrapping his arms around her. She dozed, secure in the knowledge that she had just made love with her mate. Her one true love, whom she would be proud to claim in front of her Clan and the world.

When she woke a short time later, snuggled side by side in the big bed, they talked. The mood was mellow and the words spoken in quiet tones, as if they were the only two awake at this time of night. Perhaps, they were, or perhaps, other lovers, in other places, were enjoying the same blissful interlude of peace between matched souls.

"I was truly afraid I'd lost my beast forever," Seamus admitted in the dim light of the cabin, where the setting was intimate and honest. "I thought the menagerie had broken him and that he might never heal, but I think you had a lot to do with helping me find him again, Moira."

"Me? But it was Lyn who gave you the sapling," she tried to protest, but he stilled her words with a kiss. When he let her up for air long moments later, he was smiling in that way that melted her bones.

"Lyn might've triggered something with the plant," he told her, "but it was you who healed my soul, Moira. You're my mate. Only you could've made me whole again."

"Mates, eh?" she repeated the word, savoring the feel of it. Something slid into place inside her heart, never to be dislodged. She felt happier than she ever had, all because of Seamus.

"If you'll have me," he said, turning to look deep into her eyes. "I love you, Moira."

"Oh, Seamus. I love you too." Her admission was whispered, heartfelt and final. She would never say those words to another man. Only Seamus. Her mate. The perfect partner to her soul.

"So, does that mean you'll be mine?" He seemed in doubt, so she rushed to clarify.

"Yes, Seamus. I acknowledge that you're my mate too, and that I want to spend the rest of my days with you." She kissed him joyfully, then pulled back. "I want you to meet my family, though, and they can be somewhat intimidating. We can wait until we're more settled to do that, if you want."

The last thing she wanted to do was scare him off by overwhelming him with Kinkaids. While her immediate family were selkies, there were more than a few lions in her lineage, including Samson, the king of lions himself. She knew he could be scary to the uninitiated, but he was also a bit of a pussy cat to those he loved and had sworn to protect. Seamus would learn that…eventually, but she'd give him all the time he needed to come to terms with the Clan he was about to marry into.

"I want you to meet my people too, but it'll require a rather long airplane ride. Have you ever been to Australia before?" His smile lit her world.

"No, I haven't, but I'd like to see it. With you." She kissed him gently then, lingering over the non-verbal communication that said

I love you with every stroke of lips and tongue.

A long time later, Seamus picked up the thread of their conversation.

"You know, I wasn't sure I'd ever want to go back to Oz. If my furry side hadn't come back, I wouldn't have even considered it, but he's at home there, and I have family there and responsibilities, though they've made do without me now for some time."

She had a sudden thought. "Does your family know what happened to you?"

"Yes. That was one of the first things John helped me with, getting in touch with my sister and her mate. She wanted to come, but she's expecting her first child, and I told her not to travel, that I was fine. She should be having the little one any day now, in fact." He stroked Moira's hair with tender affection. "I call her every week. She and the rest of the family know where I am, but that I have a few things to settle here before I can go home. And now that I've found you…well, we're going to have to talk about where we want to settle and how we can make this work logistically. You live in Texas, don't you?"

She nodded. "I do, but I want to be wherever you are, Seamus. I'm not sure about Australia, but I'll give it a try, if you want."

"I'd like to visit and meet my new niece or nephew, but I'm not sure I can retake the place I left. What would you say if we stayed here, in Grizzly Cove, at least for a little while?" He seemed to really want to stay with the bears, and she could be of use here too, at least for the foreseeable future.

"It's a good place to start," she agreed. "I'd like to get to know the mer better, and I bet Sam will be happy to have me continue to act as Kinkaid ambassador to Nansee's pod."

"And I still have an interest in helping find those who captured me and Eamon and his sister. I feel like I need to stay here until that situation is resolved, at least. And I'd like to help more in the search," Seamus added. "We can travel to Texas so I can meet your people any time you like."

"Are you sure?" She looked up at him. "They can be a little intimidating—even to me."

"Nothing intimidates me as long as you're by my side. With you, Moira, I feel invincible."

He kissed her and they didn't speak again

for a long, long time. They had much more pleasurable pursuits in mind.

# # #

ABOUT THE AUTHOR

Bianca D'Arc has run a laboratory, climbed the corporate ladder in the shark-infested streets of lower Manhattan, studied and taught martial arts, and earned the right to put a whole bunch of letters after her name, but she's always enjoyed writing more than any of her other pursuits. She grew up and still lives on Long Island, where she keeps busy with an extensive garden, several aquariums full of very demanding fish, and writing her favorite genres of paranormal, fantasy and sci-fi romance.

Bianca loves to hear from readers and can be reached via Facebook (BiancaDArcAuthor) or through the various links on her website.

WELCOME TO THE D'ARC SIDE…

WWW.BIANCADARC.COM

OTHER BOOKS
BY BIANCA D'ARC

Paranormal Romance

Brotherhood of Blood
One & Only
Rare Vintage
Phantom Desires
Sweeter Than Wine
Forever Valentine
Wolf Hills*
Wolf Quest

Tales of the Were
Lords of the Were
Inferno
Rocky
Slade

Tales of the Were ~ Redstone Clan
The Purrfect Stranger
Grif
Red
Magnus
Bobcat
Matt

Tales of the Were ~ String of Fate
Cat's Cradle
King's Throne
Jacob's Ladder
Her Warriors

Tales of the Were ~ Grizzly Cove
All About the Bear
Mating Dance
Night Shift
Alpha Bear
Saving Grace
Bearliest Catch
The Bear's Healing Touch
The Luck of the Shifters

Guardians of the Dark
Half Past Dead
Once Bitten, Twice Dead
A Darker Shade of Dead
The Beast Within
Dead Alert

Gifts of the Ancients: Warrior's Heart

Epic Fantasy Erotic Romance

Dragon Knights
Maiden Flight*
The Dragon Healer
Border Lair
Master at Arms
The Ice Dragon**
Prince of Spies***
Wings of Change
FireDrake
Dragon Storm
Keeper of the Flame
Hidden Dragons
The Sea Captain's Daughter Trilogy
Book 1: Sea Dragon
Book 2: Dragon Fire
Book 3: Dragon Mates

Science Fiction Romance

StarLords
Hidden Talent
Talent For Trouble
Shy Talent

Jit'Suku Chronicles ~ Arcana

King of Swords

King of Cups

King of Clubs

King of Stars

End of the Line

Diva

Jit'Suku Chronicles ~ Sons of Amber

Angel in the Badlands

Master of Her Heart

Futuristic Erotic Romance

Resonance Mates

Hara's Legacy**

Davin's Quest

Jaci's Experiment

Grady's Awakening

Harry's Sacrifice

* RT Book Reviews Awards Nominee

** EPPIE Award Winner

*** CAPA Award Winner

WWW.BIANCADARC.COM

Made in the USA
San Bernardino, CA
01 April 2017